PLANET OF THE APES

AN UNOFFICIAL COMPANION

PLANET OF THE APES

AN UNOFFICIAL COMPANION

DAVID HOFSTEDE

ECW PRESS

NATIONAL LIBRARY OF CANADA CATALOGUING IN PUBLICATION DATA

Hofstede, David
Planet of the apes: an unofficial companion

ISBN 1-55022-446-8

1. Planet of the apes films. 2. Planet of the apes (Television program). I. Title.

PN1995.9.P495H63 2001   791.43'75   C00933257-X
PR9199.3.B76C65 2001

Cover and text design by Tania Craan
Cover photo by Photofest
Layout by Mary Bowness

Printed by Webcom

Distributed in Canada by
General Distribution Services, 325 Humber College Blvd.,
Toronto, ON, M9W 7C3, Canada
Distributed in United States by
LPC GROUP, 1436 West Randolph Street, Chicago, Illinois, U.S.A. 60607
Distributed in Europe by
Turnaround Publisher Services, Unit 3, Olympia Trading Estate,
Coburg Road, Wood Green, London N2Z 6TZ
Distributed in Australia by
Wakefield Press, 17 Rundle St., Kent Town, South Australia 5071

Published by ECW PRESS
2120 Queen Street East, Suite 200
Toronto, ON M4E 1E2
ecwpress.com

This book is set in Akzidenz Grotesk and Minion.

PRINTED AND BOUND IN CANADA

The publication of Planet of the Apes has been generously supported by the Government of
Canada through the Book Publishing Industry Development Program.

Canada

ACKNOWLEDGMENTS

The author wishes to thank the following people for their help and support: Lance Clement, Don Pedro Colley, Jack Condon, Henry Corden, Jack David, Terry Hoknes, Kim Hunter, Scott Hutchins, Anthony James, Jeff Krueger, Edward Lakso, the Motion Picture Academy Library, and Ken Taylor.

TABLE OF CONTENTS

CHAPTER ONE

THE MAN WHO STARTED IT ALL
Pierre Boulle

Every motion picture, television series, cartoon, novel, and comic book about *Planet of the Apes* share one common trait: they all carry the credit line "Based on characters created by Pierre Boulle." Were it not for Boulle's original idea of a topsy-turvy world where apes rule over humans, there would be no Cornelius and Zira, no Statue of Liberty buried on the beach, no Taylor and Nova, no Burke, Virdon, or Galen. But no one was more surprised by the *Apes* phenomenon than Boulle, a French writer of adventure stories who considered his 1963 novel *Monkey Planet* (*La Planète des Singes*) one of his lesser works.

Pierre Boulle was born February 20, 1912, in Avignon, France. The son of an attorney, young Pierre craved romance and adventure. He earned a degree in engineering from the Ecole Supérieur d'Electricité, and in the 1930s he journeyed to Kuala Lampur in Malaysia, to work on a rubber plantation. During World War II, as Germany marched across Europe, Boulle became an undercover agent and resistance fighter in Indo-China. Operating under the name Peter John Rule, a Mauritius-born Englishman, Boulle helped to organize the resistance movement in Burma and China.

In 1943, he set out for Hanoi in Vietnam by floating down the Mekong River on a raft, but en route he was captured by the Vichy government, and turned over to the Japanese. Boulle was sentenced to "hard labor for life." During his incarceration, he kept a diary on scraps of paper; the observations and anecdotes he recorded would later turn up in his literary work.

After two years in a prison camp, Boulle was liberated by his captors just as the Allies closed in on victory. He spent the rest of the war with Special Forces in Calcutta, India. After a brief return to the rubber plantation, Boulle went back to France to begin work as a writer. *William Conrad*, his first novel, was published in 1950. He was 38 years old and had no literary training, but Boulle's story of secret agents in England had a firsthand authenticity that earned critical praise.

His next novel, *Bridge on the River Kwai* (1952), was Boulle's biggest commercial success. Inspired by his wartime experiences, he wrote a fictional account of Allied prisoners of war at a Japanese prison camp in Southeast Asia who are forced to build a bridge for their captors. Director David Lean adapted the book into a feature film in 1957. The movie earned six Academy Awards, including Best Picture and Best Screenplay.

Pierre Boulle was credited with writing the script, though many believed at the time that this was not the case. "Sam Spiegel, the producer, David Lean, the director, and Carl Foreman and myself worked on the screenplay. But they decided that since a great deal of the picture was based on the book and much of the dialogue had been taken right out of the book, I should get the credit for the screenplay," said Boulle in 1958. "The majority agreed most of the work was mine." However, several years later it was revealed that the script had actually been written by Carl Foreman and Michael Wilson, who posthumously received the Academy Award for their work in 1985. Said Hollywood historian Larry Caplair, "Everyone knew Boulle couldn't speak English, let alone write it."

You can tell right away that *Monkey Planet* is science fiction, because the French have a space program. The novel opens with the discovery of a bottle floating in the sea of space, by two interstellar travelers, Jinn and Phyllis. The bottle contains a plea for help from French journalist Ulysee Merou, who had accompanied a team of astronauts on an expedition in the year 2500. The memoir details his experiences on a planet where humans are treated like animals by civilized, talking apes. Merou is captured and taken to a futuristic city, where he arouses the wrath of the orangutan Dr. Zaius.

Merou falls in love with Nova, a primitive mute human with whom he has a son. Zira, a chimpanzee scientist, defends the astronaut to Zaius, which creates feelings of jealousy and rage in her friend and fellow scientist, Cornelius. The kindly Cornelius portrayed by Roddy McDowall in the movie bears little resemblance to the character's counterpart in the novel, who plots to kill Merou. Eventually, Merou, Nova, and their infant child are sent back to earth. They land at Orly Airport in Paris, where the book ends with a marvelous double twist, one that is entirely different from any revelations that appeared in the *Planet of the Apes* films.

Bridge on the River Kwai and *Monkey Planet* were Boulle's two best-sellers, but he wrote more than 30 novels and short stories in his prolific career, most of them adventure/espionage tales that shared themes of moral uncertainty. His other works include *Face of a Hero* (1953), *The Test* (1955), *A Noble Profession* (1960), and *Ears of the Jungle* (1972). He also published two memoirs, *My Own River Kwai* in 1966 and *L'Îlon* in 1991.

Pierre Boulle was appointed a chevalier of the Legion of Honor for his literary achievements. His wartime heroism earned him the Croix de Guerre and a Medal of the Resistance. Boulle died on January 30, 1994, at the age of 81. In the London Times obituary, his books were praised as superior to the films they spawned. "If he had a defect it was that he was a writer in the tradition of the French novelist of ideas, and there was a tendency for his characters to become vehicles for those ideas. But nothing he did ever fell below the level of highly intelligent entertainment."

CHAPTER TWO

APES AT THE MOVIES

The transition of Pierre Boulle's futuristic novel into a motion picture franchise began with producer Arthur P. Jacobs, a former publicist whose clients included Judy Garland, Marilyn Monroe, and Gregory Peck. Jacobs's first foray into filmmaking was in developing a script called *What a Way to Go!* for Monroe, who died before filming was completed. The project was ultimately made with Shirley Maclaine in 1964, and Jacobs enjoyed the production side of the business enough to change careers.

While working to bring the musical *Doctor Dolittle* (1967) to the screen, Jacobs went to Paris to meet with literary agents, in search of new material. Asked what type of film he'd like to make, he said, "I wish *King Kong* hadn't been made so I could make it." A few months later, one of the agents sent him a copy of Boulle's *Monkey Planet*, figuring one ape story is as good as another.

Jacobs loved the story, and purchased the screen rights. With J. Lee Thompson, the director of his first film, he drafted a five-page story treatment in which *Monkey Planet* was retitled *Planet of the Apes*. He took this pitch to MGM, Paramount, and other major studios, hoping to sign a deal that would have the film in theaters by the spring or summer of 1964. He found no takers, though he probably heard a lot of bad monkey jokes.

After months of follow-up meetings, the rights were purchased by Warner Bros. as the next production of Blake Edwards, best known for the successful *Pink Panther* series with Peter Sellers. Edwards's first task was to contact Rod Serling about writing the screenplay.

The story of human astronauts hunted by civilized apes was a natural for Serling, the man who created *The Twilight Zone* and was one of the most respected screenwriters in the industry. For the next two years, while Jacobs tried to secure funding for the budget, Serling tried various methods to adapt Boulle's book into a workable script.

Among the myriad decisions Serling faced was how much of the book would — or should — wind up on the screen. Boulle's "message in a bottle" scenario was reluctantly discarded in favor of stranding a team of astronauts, led by a character named Thomas (later changed to Taylor), on an unknown, desolate planet. Once the humans are captured by the apes, Serling's script keeps many of Boulle's characters and ideas, expanding upon the theme of uncertainty over which society came first — human or simian.

Serling originally conceived of the apes' civilization as described by Boulle. He wrote of "stores with ape mannequins in the windows," "a gorilla policeman directing traffic past a movie marquee with a large picture in front of two monkeys in a passionate embrace." But building a modern, technologically sophisticated ape city would prove too costly.

Michael Wilson, who Arthur Jacobs brought in to work on the script with Serling (though the two writers never actually met), adapted the setting to the Gaudi-esque village we see in the finished film. It is ironic, however, that Wilson's village had to be built from scratch on the Fox backlot, which also wasn't cheap. How much more could it have cost to transport a few busloads of apes to a major metropolitan city, and shoot *Planet of the Apes* in a way that was true to the novel?

Wilson also added several humorous verbal exchanges to the script, such as the oft-quoted lines "Human see, human do" and "I never met an ape I didn't like." The famous "see no evil, hear no evil, speak no evil" moment in Taylor's trial is sometimes attributed to Wilson, but was actually improvised on the set at the suggestion of Charlton Heston and Mort Abrahams.

The climax of Serling's final draft, which he submitted to Jacobs in 1965, featured a change from previous efforts, which ended with Taylor and Nova escaping the planet and returning to "earth," only to find it now inhabited by apes (a similar ending to Boulle's book). Subsequent drafts had Taylor escaping by helicopter, and seeing the Statue of Liberty from the air; in another version, Taylor is killed by gorilla soldiers, and carried past the Statue as the film ends. In Serling's final draft, he kept the Statue of Liberty, but had Taylor and Nova ride toward it on horseback.

At various times both Serling and Wilson have taken credit for the film's now classic denouement. But Serling's authorship has been backed by Mort Abrahams, and seems reasonable given the many similar twist endings that were a staple on the writer's *Twilight Zone* series. Fans of the show may recall an episode entitled "I Shot an Arrow into the Air," written by Serling in 1959 (four years before Boulle's novel was published). In it, a crew of astronauts crash on an unknown desert planet, and turn on each other. After two members of the team are killed, the others realize they've been on earth all the time.

While the writers fine-tuned the film's story, Arthur Jacobs began the process of casting. His original plan to interest Marlon Brando in a lead role hadn't panned out, but he was determined that the role of Taylor be filled by a big-name star. His list of prospects included Burt Lancaster, Paul Newman, Jack Lemmon, and Rock Hudson. They all turned him down, so Jacobs contacted Charlton Heston, who was intrigued by the idea.

Though Heston was already famous for his portrayals of larger-than-life heroes in such cinematic epics as *The Ten Commandments* (1956), *Ben Hur* (1959), and *El Cid* (1961), he was (and still is) an actor willing to take risks with offbeat roles. Today, *Planet of the Apes* is a science fiction classic, but nobody knew that in 1965, and there was every chance that the sight of

Kim Hunter, who played the only blue-eyed chimpanzee on earth in the first three *Planet of the Apes* films (Globe Photos).

Heston being chased around the screen by talking apes might shorten his distinguished career.

Both Shirley Maclaine and Julie Harris were approached to play Dr. Zira, but the role ultimately went to Kim Hunter, a former client of Arthur Jacobs from his days as a publicist, and an Academy Award winner for her portrayal of Stella Kowalski in *A Streetcar Named Desire* (1951). "My agent called and said he had a script to send me," she recalls. "I read it, and told them I was interested. A couple of weeks went by, then I got a call from someone in the casting department, who asked 'Ms. Hunter, how tall are you?' I thought that was an odd question. But I said 5'3", and they said 'Thank you very much' and hung up. They wanted to make sure I was short enough to play a chimp, in relation to the human beings."

Roddy McDowall would join Kim Hunter in the chimp makeup as Cornelius, and Edward G. Robinson signed on to play the enigmatic orangutan Dr. Zaius, after the role was turned down by Peter Ustinov. Jacobs's first choice for Nova was Ursula Andress, who had spent her entire film career in a bikini. Angelique Pettyjohn, best known as the green-haired babe in the *Star Trek* episode "The Gamesters of Triskelion," also filmed a screen test. Then Jacobs toyed with the idea of launching an international talent search for a beautiful young woman, to generate free publicity for the movie. But when Twentieth Century Fox studio chief Richard Zanuck gave *Planet of the Apes* the go-ahead to start production, the role of Nova went to raven-haired beauty Linda Harrison, a former Miss Maryland, and the future Mrs. Zanuck.

Delays in finding a studio and securing a start date prevented J. Lee Thompson from directing the film he helped conceive, though he would later return to the *Apes* series and direct the final two installments. Veteran directors Fritz Lang, Mervyn LeRoy, Sydney Pollack, and Irvin Kershner were considered, but it was Charlton Heston who suggested Franklin Schaffner, with whom he had recently worked in *The War Lord* (1965).

One of the aforementioned delays was caused when Warner Bros. passed on the *Apes* film, after the projected budget topped $7 million. Blake Edwards dropped out as well, and Richard Zanuck dropped in, but not without reservations. Since the entire plot hinged on the believability of a race of intelligent apes,

Zanuck wanted to make certain that audiences would accept the premise by ordering a makeup test.

On March 8, 1966, a five-minute film was shot at Twentieth Century Fox, at a cost of $5,000. The script for the one-scene test was written by Rod Serling, and featured Charlton Heston, and Edward G. Robinson as Dr. Zaius. Two Fox contract players, James Brolin and Linda Harrison, played the roles of Cornelius and Zira, but were not made up as apes. Makeup artist Ben Nye transformed Robinson into Zaius, who appears not as a completely simian creature, but more of an ape-human hybrid. There were no prosthetics used on his face, which retained his human hairline and forehead. Cinnamon-brown fur whiskers on his cheeks protruded outward, like a long mustache.

Though the makeup was not as sophisticated as what ultimately appeared in the film, it was enough to convince Zanuck that the movie would work. It was also enough to convince Edward G. Robinson to quit the film, citing health concerns and a reluctance to endure the transformations over a period of months. Maurice Evans, then known to television audiences as Maurice, Samantha's father on *Bewitched*, would play Zaius in the first two *Apes* films.

Richard Zanuck told Arthur Jacobs and Mort Abrahams that he still had reservations about spending $7 million on a science fiction film with such a bizarre premise. But when *Fantastic Voyage* (1966) opened to good reviews and big business, Zanuck decided that another sci-fi gamble might also pay off. So in one sense, the *Planet of the Apes* series and all the subsequent adaptations that followed, owe their very existence to Raquel Welch's breast-stroke through the human bloodstream in a tight, white jumpsuit.

Three years after Jacobs first read *Monkey Planet*, he finally had a deal in place; Fox would make *Planet of the Apes* if it could be completed on a budget of $5 million. Jacobs agreed, realizing that 20 percent of that amount might be devoted to makeup alone. "I knew what they wanted, and I knew it could be done. But I also had an idea of what it was going to cost, and nobody in the history of filmmaking had ever spent that much money on makeup!" said John Chambers, who was hired to turn dozens of actors and extras into three different species of apes.

But Chambers got what he needed — an unprecedented makeup budget of $1 million. Months of research followed; Chambers had no template to start from, as previous films featuring apes all used some variation on the basic monkey suit worn by revelers at Halloween parties. He progressed from drawings to sculpted molds, to find a look that would be convincing, even in close-ups. He also utilized skills he learned while designing prosthetic limbs for wounded soldiers in veterans' hospitals. Chambers had earlier employed variations on these prosthetics to create creatures for *The Munsters*, *The Outer Limits*, and *Lost in Space*, and for Mr. Spock's ears on *Star Trek*.

Since the *Apes* performers would be encased in their makeup, sometimes for 12–18 hours a day, Chambers created a special foam rubber with simulated "pores," which allowed the actors to perspire through the appliances, rather than underneath them. It helped — but not much. "When I got done with that first test, putting the appliances on me, I went back to the hotel and got drunk — I couldn't believe I would have to do that every day," recalled Kim Hunter. "I don't like pills, but I went to my doctor and described to him what I went through. I told him I needed something just to get me through the makeup sessions, but after that I need to be alert; he gave me valium. After a week or so, I said, 'Oh, I don't need to take those any more, I can get through it.' But the next day, I fussed so much that my makeup artist said, 'You better take those drugs!'"

The actors had some free movement of their faces, which helped them to manipulate the prosthetics and give their simian characters facial expressions. "Arthur [Jacobs] would say 'You've got to keep the face moving,'" said Hunter. "Normally when you listen to somebody else you don't move your face muscles much, but for the camera, if you don't move your face, it looks like a mask. So we were moving those muscles like crazy, all the time."

Roddy McDowall with makeup artist Fred Blau, before (top) and after (Globe Photos).

Voice projection was another challenge: "There was a slight problem because we were so hidden behind the appliances. We tended to sound nasal. They sent Roddy and me off to a room to read things and talk to each other, and find a way to solve the problem. We found we had to deliberately send the sound into our upper palate but very far forward, and if we were very careful we lost the nasality. Then we had to teach everybody else how to do it," Hunter remembers.

Korean hair was used on the appliances for its texture; the budget for the hair used on the apes' faces, hands, and arms topped $75,000 alone. All the apes were given brown eyes — blue-eyed actors were fitted for brown contact lenses, except for Kim Hunter, who was allowed to remain blue-eyed. Chambers said "We all thought it would add a human touch." Once complete, the masks had to be painted. This was a delicate, meticulous process, and special care had to be taken to assure that the exact color shades for each character would match from day to day.

Fox opened a temporary school to train 200 makeup artists, and borrowed as many as could be spared from other productions. As a result, several other films in 1967 suffered delays in their shooting schedules, because all the makeup people in town were over on *Planet of the Apes*.

All together, the process of converting an actor into an ape took between three and four hours, every day. Since the appliances could not be removed for meals, the actors sipped beverages and soft foods like apple sauce through a straw. "The only thing we couldn't do was blow our noses," said Lou Wagner, who played Lucius. Roddy McDowall failed to heed this sound advice, when he sneezed one day and blew half his face off.

From the moment filming began on May 21, 1967, tight security was the rule on the set, to protect the movie's secrets. Back in the days before *Entertainment Tonight* and *Entertainment Weekly*, it was actually possible to surprise an audience with a bold new filmmaking vision, and Arthur Jacobs was determined to keep his movie to himself until it was released.

Separate makeup and commissary facilities were set up on the three sound stages where the film was shot. A memo issued by Jacobs ordered that "All actors who appear as apes will be made up and dressed on the stages and will have lunch catered to them in specially designed and staffed eating areas. No actor in makeup will be permitted off the set during the working day." Kim Hunter discovered the extent of the security firsthand. "One day I finished early and I came back to the lot, to see everybody before I went home, and they wouldn't let me in! I finally got somebody to say, 'She's in it. She doesn't look like it now, but she's in it.'"

A writer from the *Hollywood Reporter* received a sneak preview of the ape village, and described it as "the wildest looking movie set this town has seen since Lon Chaney first scared the daylights out of Hollywood when he made *The Hunchback of Notre Dame.*" The reporter also published the film's amusing work schedule sheets: "Limousine — pick up gorillas at 8 a.m. Lunch break for chimpanzees at noon."

But there were stranger happenings than that going on, that were not revealed until after the film was released. A sociologist could write a thesis on the self-segregation that occurred on the set among the actors who played chimpanzees, gorillas, and orangutans. "It was a question of getting close to those who understood what you were going through," explained Kim Hunter, who always ate with her fellow chimps. Though she and Maurice Evans were close friends, they rarely spoke during breaks in production, because they had joined different species.

Cast members who played humans, like Charlton Heston, never saw their simian costars without their makeup. The first time Heston saw Kim Hunter as herself, he didn't recognize her. Thirty years later, when American Movie Classics hosted a special anniversary screening of *Planet of the Apes*, he made the same mistake. "I said hi to him and he just said 'hello' and kept going," she remembered. "Finally someone made him realize who I was, and he came back and said, 'My God, I still can't connect you to that role.'"

Filming was completed on August 10, 1967; budget restrictions had forced a cut in the shooting scheduled from 55 to 45 days. Post-production progressed smoothly, after one minor quibble with the Motion Picture Code was resolved. There was some concern over Taylor's admonition of "God damn you" in the final scene. Arthur Jacobs convinced the censors to allow it, since the expression was not intended as a profane epithet, but a literal expression of Taylor's feelings — he was calling on God to damn the men who destroyed civilization.

As the movie's February 8, 1968 premiere approached, cast and crew alike wondered what kind of reception *Planet of the Apes* would receive. "I remember John Chambers said early on, 'it's going to be very interesting to see how people respond to it,'" said Kim Hunter. "Either we're going to have enough reality so the audience can reach us, and we can reach them, or it's going to be Mickey Mouse. We didn't know, really."

PLANET OF THE APES
(Twentieth Century Fox, 1968)

Directed by Franklin J. Schaffner; Written by Michael Wilson and Rod Serling (based on the novel *Monkey Planet* by Pierre Boulle); Produced by Arthur P. Jacobs; Photographed by Leon Shamroy; Music by Jerry Goldsmith; Edited by Hugh S. Fowler; Art direction by Jack Martin Smith and William Creber; Set decoration by Walter M. Scott and Norman Rockett; Costumes by Morton Haack; Special effects by L. B. Abbott, Art Cruickshank, and Emil Kosa, Jr.; Makeup by John Chambers, Ben Nye, and Dan Striepeke.

CAST:

Charlton Heston (George Taylor)
Roddy McDowall (Cornelius)
Kim Hunter (Dr. Zira)
Maurice Evans (Dr. Zaius)
James Whitmore (President of the Assembly)
James Daly (Honorius)
Linda Harrison (Nova)
Robert Gunner (Landon)
Lou Wagner (Lucius)
Woodrow Parfrey (Maximus)
Jeff Burton (Dodge)
Buck Kartalian (Julius)
Norman Burton (Hunt Leader)
Wright King (Dr. Galen)
Paul Lambert (Minister)
Dianne Stanley (Female Astronaut)

REVIEWS:

"By its appeal to both the imagination and the intellect within a context of action and elemental adventure, in its relevance to the consuming issues of its time, by the means with which it provides maximum entertainment . . . *Planet of the Apes* is that rare film which will transcend all age and social groupings." (*Hollywood Reporter*)

"The best American movie I have seen so far this year." (*Life*)

"*Planet of the Apes* is that rarity, a Hollywood blockbuster that not only attempts much but actually accomplishes all that it set out to do. A triumph of artistry and imagination." (*Los Angeles Times*)

"Interesting in a boring sort of way. The central situation is attractive and the physical details are ingenious, but the story development is unaspiring and the dialogue stultifying." (*The Nation*)

"It is no good at all, but fun, at moments, to watch." (*New York Times*)

"This is one of the most entertaining science fiction fantasies to ever come out of Hollywood. Heston is a godlike hero; built for strength, he's an archetype of what makes Americans win." (Pauline Kael, *The New Yorker*)

"The surprise ending proves that the picture had some serious things on its mind all along. But such big things to have on such a little mind!" (*Newsweek*)

"On the screen the story has been reduced from Swiftian satire to self-parody. . . . The best thing about the film results from producer Arthur P. Jacobs's decision to allocate $1,000,000 for masks and costumes." (*Time*)

"*Planet of the Apes* is an amazing film. A political-sociological allegory, cast in the mold of futuristic science fiction, the [production] is an intriguing blend of chilling satire, a sometimes ludicrous juxtaposition of human and ape mores, optimism and pessimism." (*Variety*)

THE BALANCE SHEET:

Planet of the Apes was made for $5.8 million; the film ranked #6 on *Variety*'s box-office chart for 1968, earning $15 million in its original release.

AWARDS:

Planet of the Apes earned Academy Award nominations for Best Costume Design and Best Original Score. John Chambers received an honorary Oscar for Outstanding Achievement in Makeup.

WHAT IT'S ABOUT:

Four astronauts near the end of a six-month mission through deep space. Because time passes differently during their journey, they expect to return to earth in the year 2673. Taylor, the mission commander, wonders if man will have become more civilized in the future, or if he "still keeps his brother starving."

The spaceship develops mechanical problems, and crash-lands in 3978 on an unknown planet in the constellation of Orion. The three crewmen who survive the crash search for signs of life, and find a tribe of primitive humans being pursued by apes on horseback. Taylor, rendered unable to speak by a throat wound, can only watch in horror as he is captured by the intelligent apes, and thrown into a cage. The other astronauts suffer more dire fates: one is killed, the other lobotomized.

Taylor and a female human, whom he names "Nova," are put in the custody of the chimpanzee scientist Dr. Zira; both are slated for medical experiments. Zira is astonished when Taylor shows unusual signs of intelligence, an unexpected circumstance on a world where men are treated like animals. When Taylor finally speaks, he is turned over to Dr. Zaius, chief scientist and orangutan leader.

Taylor is put on trial, but escapes with the help of Zira and her fiancé, Cornelius. They flee into the "Forbidden Zone," a desert surrounding the city, where Cornelius has unearthed artifacts

"Zaius . . . it's third and long." During a break in shooting *Planet of the Apes*, Charlton Heston shows off his quarter-back skills (Globe Photos).

from an early, pre-ape civilization that Zaius wants suppressed. But after a brief battle, Zaius allows Taylor and Nova to leave on their own, though he warns that they may not like what they find. On a beach, Taylor is stunned to see the remains of the Statue of Liberty, buried in the sand. He had been on earth all the time.

THE QUOTABLE APES:

"I can't help thinking that somewhere in the universe there has to be something better than man." (Taylor)

"You know what they say — human see, human do." (Julius)

"Take your stinking paws off me you damn dirty ape!" (Taylor)

"You finally, really did it — you maniacs! You blew it up! Damn you! Damn you all to hell!" (Taylor)

WHAT'S GREAT ABOUT IT:

Actually, just about everything is great about *Planet of the Apes*, one of the most perfectly realized science fiction films in the history of the medium. Its praises were sung by such distinguished film critics as the *New Yorker*'s Pauline Kael, who raved that "At times, [*Planet*] has the primitive force of old King Kong." Audiences cheered with equal enthusiasm, and haven't stopped for more than a quarter-century.

Planet of the Apes has earned well-deserved praise for almost every aspect of its production, from the remarkable simian makeup created by John Chambers to its intelligent script rich in irony and symbolism, and the fine performances of Charlton Heston, Kim Hunter, Roddy McDowall, and Maurice Evans. It's a film of escalating surprises, that saves its best revelation — that incredible, shattering final scene — for last.

Director Franklin Schaffner sets the story in motion with deliberate patience, favoring long, sweeping camera shots of the astronauts after they land on a mysterious planet. By depicting

Taylor and his crew as small moving figures in grand vistas of empty, rugged terrain, Schaffner reinforces their isolation, and their vulnerability. The first glimpse of the apes does not occur until 32 minutes into the film; the particulars of ape society are gradually unveiled by degrees, through the eyes of Taylor. On a basic level the movie is simple role reversal — apes are the dominant evolved species, men are kept in cages — and *Planet of the Apes* is thoroughly entertaining on that level. But it's the deeper meanings, some subtly expressed, others practically a call to arms, that have kept the film so firmly rooted in the public consciousness.

🐒 Timeless themes. The science fiction genre does not traditionally date well, as the present inevitably catches up with the futuristic visions of movies made decades in the past. But the political and sociological messages of *Planet of the Apes* haven't become dated, which is not necessarily a good thing. Sadly, society in the 21st century still struggles with war, race relations, class conflict, church inquisition, the credibility gap in official statements of position, and blind allegiance to the status quo. In 1967, the film's depiction of intolerance could be interpreted as a comment on the Civil Rights movement, but racial tension still hasn't gone away, whether it's blacks and whites in America or Arabs and Jews in the Middle East. "The apes didn't understand the human beings, and didn't want anything to do with them. The problem is worldwide — being afraid of people that aren't like you, or don't come from the same background," said Kim Hunter. The horrible policy of ethnic cleansing, suggested by Zaius and revived by General Ursus in *Beneath*, suggested Vietnam when the films were released, but a viewer watching the movies now might think of Bosnia or Rwanda.

🐒 Racism among apes. Where a less ambitious creature feature would have been content with an "us vs. them" conflict of apes and humans, *Planet of the Apes* depicts parochialism within ape society as well. Dr. Zaius and his fellow orangutans look down upon the pacifist chimpanzees, and Zira's compassion for Taylor confuses the orangutans and repels the gorilla soldiers, who see human beings only as dumb animals that cannot be trusted.

🐾 A misanthrope as protagonist. Astronaut Taylor is hardly the standard action movie hero. His cynical, caustic diatribes against the human race are exemplified by the scene in which he laughs when told his family and friends have been dead for 200 centuries. Subsequent events force Taylor to defend humanity to his ape captors, only to have his worst fears realized by . . .

🐾 The legendary final scene. Only the film adaptation of Stephen King's *Carrie* (1976) gives viewers a bigger jolt just before the closing credits. But where *Carrie*'s final "appearance" offered only shock value, Taylor's reaction to the Statue of Liberty in *Planet of the Apes* is far more resonant. The revelation that Taylor had been on earth all along reshapes and intensifies everything that had happened previously. And though any recognizable landmark — Big Ben, the Eiffel Tower, McDonald's — would have revealed Taylor's location with equal precision, the choice of the Statue of Liberty, a symbol of hope and pride and all that is good about the human race, makes the discovery even more devastating.

Only Pierre Boulle found the climax disappointing. In a memo to Arthur Jacobs, he wrote, "I have come to consider [the ending] as a temptation from the devil. I am definitely against it, from every point of view."

🐾 Hidden meanings. Writer Michael Wilson was blacklisted during the Joseph McCarthy era of Hollywood communist witch-hunts. He utilized that experience in the trial sequence of *Planet of the Apes*, in which Taylor stands accused by the ape council, but no charge is levied.

🐾 The astronauts' spaceship. It's a classic 1960s' style craft, with clean lines and elegant design, and a big black leather office chair at the helm, reminiscent of the first Enterprise in *Star Trek*. It's hard to believe that the pointed nose of the craft, still visible after the crash, was made of plywood. The same ship was used in the first episode of the *Planet of the Apes* television series.

🦍 The way Kim Hunter's Zira says "Cor-NEL-ius!" with a bemusing mix of love and exasperation.

🦍 Jerry Goldsmith's score. To this day, it's hard to hear a ram's horn in any other film or television soundtrack, and not think of *Planet of the Apes*.

WHAT'S NOT SO GREAT:

🦍 The opening scene. The astronauts' mission, though admittedly only incidental to the plot, could be more clearly defined. It takes repeat viewings to figure out exactly what they're supposed to be doing, how long they're supposed to be gone, and how much farther into the future they unintentionally travel.

🦍 Though histrionics are part of his charm, Charlton Heston does overdo it a bit in certain scenes, particularly when Taylor is behind bars. When Heston names Nova, and later bellows, "It's a madhouse! A maaaaaad-houuuuuuse!" while getting sprayed with a fire hose, it's hard not to chuckle.

DID YOU KNOW?

🦍 Arthur Jacobs told Rod Serling that he would win an Academy Award for his *Planet of the Apes* script. Serling asked for a crate of bananas instead. The generous producer had not one, but four crates sent to the writer's residence.

🦍 The opening scenes of *Planet of the Apes* were filmed in Page, Arizona. One of the Styrofoam rocks used in the film is still on display at Page's John Wesley Powell Museum. Other outdoor scenes were shot at Malibu Creek State Park in California, which was then owned by Twentieth Century Fox. The Statue of Liberty climax was shot at Point Dune, California, at a remote section of seacoast between Malibu and Oxnard.

The head and torch of the Statue of Liberty were built at one-half full scale.

The ape village, often described as Gaudi-esque due to its similarities to the designs of Spanish architect Antonio Gaudi, was created by art director William Creber, and modeled after troglodyte ruins in Turkey.

John Chambers's honorary Academy Award for makeup was only the second time in Academy history that an Oscar was awarded for makeup (the first went to William Tuttle, for *7 Faces of Dr. Lao* in 1964). But some observers felt that the award went to the wrong movie! Stanley Kubrick's *2001: A Space Odyssey* was also released in 1968, and also featured ape-like makeup in the primitive man sequence that opens the film. Kubrick was reportedly upset by Chambers's victory, believing that *2001* deserved the special honor. At the 1968 Oscar ceremony, Chambers received his Academy Award from Walter Matthau and a chimpanzee. "Best Makeup" became a permanent Oscar category in 1981. The first recipient was Rick Baker (for his work on *An American Werewolf in London*), now the makeup supervisor on the remake of *Planet of the Apes*, released in 2001. See how this all ties together?

A severe cold affected Charlton Heston's delivery of the film's most famous line, "Take your stinking paws off me, you damn dirty ape!" However, since Taylor was suffering from exhaustion, and had just recovered from a throat injury, Heston's raw, raspy voice was just right for the moment.

Twentieth Century-Fox studio chief Richard Zanuck with wife Linda Harrison, who played Nova (Globe Photos).

Not only was Linda Harrison (Nova) Miss Maryland in the 1965 Miss America pageant, she finished as first runner-up to the winner, Arizona's Vonda Van Dyke.

A sequence showing a pregnant Nova was filmed, but cut before the movie was released, supposedly at the insistence of a Fox executive who found it "distasteful."

Roddy McDowall created the simian walk of Cornelius by combining the crouched posture of Groucho Marx with a conscious effort to mentally fuse his body between his shoulders and tail bone.

🦍 Charlton Heston drove a chariot in *Ben Hur* (1959), spent hours on his back painting the ceiling of the Sistine Chapel in *The Agony and the Ecstasy* (1965), and parted the Red Sea in *The Ten Commandments* (1956), but he described *Planet of the Apes* as the most physically arduous film he ever made. "In the first place, I was all but naked through the whole thing," he told *People* magazine in 1998. "I was fire-hosed and dragged and choked and whipped and caught in a net and held upside-down and all kinds of fun things."

🦍 On August 27, 1998, the Academy of Motion Picture Arts and Sciences hosted a 30th anniversary screening of *Planet of the Apes*. Among those in attendance were Charlton Heston, Kim Hunter, Roddy McDowall, Linda Harrison, and John Chambers. Heston, then president of the National Rifle Association, heard laughter and applause when Taylor asks for a rifle to fight the gorilla soldiers.

🦍 To promote the film's 30th anniversary, *Planet of the Apes* was screened for gorillas at the Santa Barbara Zoo. "I don't know how they'll react," said zoo spokeswoman Kelly Rogers. "I don't see them sitting down for the whole show."

🦍 A copy of the statue of the Lawgiver, which stands on the altar during the funeral scene, was given to entertainer Sammy Davis Jr. as a gift from producer Arthur Jacobs. Davis placed the statue in the garden of his Beverly Hills home.

🦍 In November of 1998, when Senator John Glenn was launched into space on a much-publicized shuttle mission, thousands of people received a joke in their e-mail box, suggesting that before Glenn returned to earth, everybody should dress in ape suits and bury the Statue of Liberty.

BENEATH THE PLANET OF THE APES
(Twentieth Century Fox, 1970)

Directed by Ted Post; Written by Paul Dehn and Mort Abrahams; Produced by Arthur P. Jacobs; Photographed by Milton Krasner; Music by Leonard Rosenman; Edited by Marion Rothman; Art direction by Jack Martin Smith and William Creber; Set direction by Walter M. Scott and Sven Wickman; Costumes by Morton Haack; Makeup by John Chambers.

CAST:

Charlton Heston (George Taylor)
James Franciscus (Brent)
Kim Hunter (Dr. Zira)
Maurice Evans (Dr. Zaius)
Linda Harrison (Nova)
Paul Richards (Mendez)
Victor Buono (Fat Man)
James Gregory (Ursus)
Jeff Corey (Caspay)
Natalie Trundy (Albina)
Thomas Gomez (Minister)
David Watson (Cornelius)
Don Pedro Colley (Negro)
Tod Andrews (Skipper)
Gregory Sierra (Gorilla Sergeant)
Lou Wagner (Lucius)

REVIEWS:

"Fortunately, there apparently can be no sequel to this current simian simile which ends with the total destruction of the world. . . . Mostly for laughs. Ten-year-olds will love it. Maybe." (*Cue*)

". . . an amusing, highly enjoyable adventure film. It lacks the moral complexity and the intellectual stimulation of its predecessor, but it is good science fiction." (*Los Angeles Herald-Examiner*)

No Chuck was good luck for James Franciscus, who played astronaut Brent in *Beneath the Planet of the Apes* (Y. Kahana/ Shooting Star).

"Striking, imaginative picture. . . . Although *Beneath the Planet of the Apes* verges upon Flash Gordon camp at times — it ends upon the starkest note any movie possibly can." (*Los Angeles Times*)

". . . pretty juvenile. *Beneath the Planet of the Apes* is not an original, but a derivative melodrama. It has a few amusing, unusual, creative scenes to its credit." (*New York Times*)

"The first of the series wasn't bad. This one very definitely is." (*Saturday Review*)

"Blown-up matinee serial, that blows up (literally), but really blew it by not deepening the concept of the original." (*Show*)

"Perhaps in the next installment . . . some of the apes could show up in Hollywood, where executive positions await them at Twentieth Century Fox." (*Time*)

"Hokey and slapdash. . . . The dialogue, acting and direction are substandard." (*Variety*)

THE BALANCE SHEET:
Beneath the Planet of the Apes was made for $3 million; the film ranked #12 on *Variety*'s box-office chart for 1970, earning $7.2 million in its original release.

WHAT IT'S ABOUT:
A search-and-rescue spaceship traces the flight trajectory followed by Taylor's lost crew, passes through the same bend in time and crash-lands on earth in the year 3955. Brent, the sole survivor of the crash, meets up with Nova, who had been traveling with Taylor until he mysteriously disappeared into a rock formation. Though she is unable to speak, Brent notices she is wearing Taylor's military I.D. tags, and hopes she will lead him to the missing astronaut.

They are captured in Ape City, but helped to escape by Cornelius and Zira. Staying just ahead of the gorilla patrols, Brent and Nova discover a subterranean cavern that used to be a New York subway station. Inside, they are accosted by a congregation of telepathic mutant humans, who have created a religion based on the worship of an unexploded nuclear missile. Brent finds Taylor, who had been imprisoned by the mutants, but their happy reunion is short-lived; the apes and the mutants wage a vicious battle, in which Brent and Nova are killed. Taylor, mortally wounded, detonates the missile, destroying the planet.

THE QUOTABLE APES:
"The only good human is a dead human." (Ursus)

"We are a peaceful people. We don't kill our enemies — we get our enemies to kill each other." (Negro)

"Zaius . . . it's doomsday." (Taylor)

WHAT'S GREAT ABOUT IT:
🐒 Brent's discovery of where he's landed, when he and Nova explore the remains of the subway station, and glimpse several familiar New York landmarks. His reaction echoes that of Taylor in *Planet of the Apes*: "My God, did we finally do it?"

🐒 Dr. Zaius's ability to see through the illusions conjured by the mutant telepaths. The scene is an apt reminder of what made him such a formidable adversary.

🐒 Nova speaks! In her second series appearance, Linda Harrison still didn't have to worry about memorizing her lines, but after keeping silent in the first film, she does utter one word, "Taylor!" during *Beneath*'s explosive climax.

🐒 The production and set design of Jack Martin Smith,

Planet of the Apes stars Natalie Trundy, Linda Harrison, and David Watson mingle with mannequins of their simian adversaries (Globe Photos).

William Creber, Walter M. Scott, and Sven Wickman. The movie's most memorable image is that of Brent and Nova wandering through the ruins of the New York Stock Exchange and Radio City Music Hall.

🐒 Nova's death. Not a cause for celebration, certainly, but one has to admire how director Ted Post handled this tragic scene, which begins without any advance set-up, and ends so quickly that by the time viewers can process what they just saw, Nova has already become the victim of a war beyond her understanding. In a movie that delivers the rest of its messages with giant, flashing, glow-in-the-dark cinematic exclamation points, it's a scene that is all the more effective for its subtlety and restraint.

WHAT'S NOT SO GREAT:

🦍 No one in the U.S. space program seems capable of landing a ship without crashing.

🦍 Departures. *Beneath* marks the final series appearances of Charlton Heston, Linda Harrison, and Maurice Evans.

🦍 Not enough Cornelius and Zira. The two winsome chimpanzees who embodied the more compassionate side of ape culture appear in only a handful of scenes. "I originally said 'no' to the sequel. Arthur had to talk me into coming back," recalls Kim Hunter. "There wasn't much of a role, but he said, 'You're Zira. Nobody else can do it.'"

🦍 No Roddy McDowall. Though he had hoped to reprise his role of Cornelius, McDowall had a prior commitment to direct *The Devil's Widow* (1972), a romantic drama starring Ava Gardner. Actor/singer David Watson portrays Cornelius instead. It has been written in various fan publications that McDowall pre-recorded some or all of the character's dialogue, but this was not the case.

🦍 James Franciscus as Brent. Cast for his remarkable resemblance to Charlton Heston — even Zira mistakes Brent for Taylor at their first meeting — Franciscus lacks his predecessor's intensity and charisma. These deficiencies are amplified by the script, in which Brent spends most of his time talking to people who won't speak — first Nova, and then the telepathic mutants. Big Chuck might have gotten away with bouncing bombastic dialogue off mute costars for 90 minutes, but Franciscus can't pull it off.

A There's not much of a story in the first hour, as audiences excited about seeing Taylor again were disappointed when the character made a mysterious, hasty exit. It is only after Brent and Nova begin following the subway tracks that the movie begins to move in a definite direction. Suspense builds in the classic tradition of the quest movie, though the pay-off is not entirely satisfying.

A Blatant symbolism. All of the *Planet of the Apes* films are immersed in political, social, and religious commentary, but *Beneath* nearly sinks under the weight of its symbolism. Scenes in which soldiers on horseback trample the peace signs of chimpanzee demonstrators are an obvious allusion to the Vietnam protest movement, and when the mutant humans sing hymns to a nuclear bomb, it's all a bit silly.

DID YOU KNOW?
A The original title for *Beneath* was *Planet of the Apes Revisited*. *Planet of the Men* was also briefly considered.

A The script for *Beneath* went through several drafts, and several different ideas were considered for its storyline. In Rod Serling's first treatment, Taylor and Nova find the remains of a city, and battle the apes that pursue them through the Forbidden Zone. They are joined by a new crew of human astronauts who followed Taylor's flight path from the past. The climax had Taylor choosing to stay on the planet with Nova, rather than return home.

Producers wanted a more explosive climax, so Serling suggested having Taylor and Nova find a spacecraft and journey to another planet, only to discover that it too was controlled by apes. He also offered an alternate story, in which the couple travel forward or backward in time.

Pierre Boulle was also approached for story ideas. Boulle submitted a script in which Taylor and Nova try to lead mankind in a battle to reclaim earth, while reducing apes back to their primitive state. The final scene depicted Dr. Zaius caged as a circus attraction.

Even the final draft, written by Paul Dehn and Mort Abrahams, originally had a different ending, in which Taylor, Nova, Cornelius, and Zira survive the nuclear explosion. They return to Ape City to establish a new order, personified by the birth of a half-human, half-ape child. An inter-species birth, however, might have threatened the films 'G' rating, so the idea was scrapped. Charlton Heston favored the ending in which nobody survived, more for its elimination of any future sequel possibilities (ha!) than its dramatic impact.

🐒 Charlton Heston had to be talked into appearing in the sequel, and once he agreed to reprise the role of Taylor, he demanded that his character be killed in the first scene. Fox studio chief Richard Zanuck eventually convinced Heston to play a slightly more substantial role in *Beneath*, but the actor refused payment for his work. His salary was donated to Harvard School, a private learning academy in Los Angeles. Both Richard Zanuck and Heston's son, Frasier, are alumni. Still, it was not an assignment he enjoyed, as he recorded in a diary he kept throughout his career: "This is the first film . . . first acting . . . I've ever done in my life for which I have no enthusiasm, which is a vital loss."

Don Pedro Colley, who played Negro, confirmed Heston's unhappiness on the set, but he had made his peace with the film when the two met again at the *Planet of the Apes* 30th anniversary screening in Los Angeles. "I went up to him at the reception and I said, 'we don't kill our enemies, we get our enemies to kill each other.' And he broke into a wonderful, wide open smile and said 'Don Pedro!' and reached out and grabbed my hand."

🐒 Burt Reynolds turned down the opportunity to play Brent.

Arthur Jacobs produced the *Planet of the Apes* film series. His wife, Natalie Trundy, appeared in four of the five films (Globe Photos).

🐒 James Franciscus thought the character of Brent was too much of a wimp, and rewrote 60 pages of the script. Most of his changes remained in the story.

🐒 Natalie Trundy, the wife of producer Arthur Jacobs, makes the first of her four series appearances in *Beneath*. Here, she plays the mutant Albina.

🐒 The "faces" of the mutants were inspired by a photograph in the medical textbook *Gray's Anatomy*. Director Ted Post advised the makeup team to create faces without an epidermis (skin covering) that would expose muscles and blood vessels. "I arrived at the makeup chair at 4:30 a.m., and by 9 a.m. I was ready to go to the set," said Don Pedro Colley. "The mold was glued to our faces, which was very uncomfortable. After 8–10 hours under the mask, my face felt like it had experienced a very intense sunburn. But I'm a character actor, and all of that was totally thrilling to me."

In several Ape City crowd scenes, most notably during General Ursus's speech, chimpanzees and orangutans were fitted with inferior ape masks to save money.

The set used for the mutant "church" was also seen as the Harmonia Gardens in the film *Hello, Dolly!* (1969).

Among serious sci-fi fanboys, the term "Franciscus" has been created to describe an inferior actor replacement, as in "Roger Moore's portrayal of James Bond was really a Franciscus." The expression can be found in the 1998 film *Free Enterprise*.

ESCAPE FROM THE PLANET OF THE APES
(Twentieth Century Fox, 1971)

Directed by Don Taylor; Written by Paul Dehn; Produced by Arthur P. Jacobs; Photographed by Joseph Biroc; Music by Jerry Goldsmith; Edited by Marion Rothman; Art direction by Jack Martin Smith and William Creber; Set direction by Walter M. Scott and Stuart A. Reiss; Special effects by the Howard A. Anderson Co.; Makeup by John Chambers and Dan Striepeke.

CAST:
Roddy McDowall (Cornelius)
Kim Hunter (Dr. Zira)
Bradford Dillman (Dr. Lewis Dixon)
Natalie Trundy (Dr. Stephanie Branton)
Eric Braeden (Dr. Otto Hasslein)
William Windom (The President)

Sal Mineo (Milo)
Albert Salmi (E-1)
Jason Evers (E-2)
John Randolph (Chairman)
Harry Lauter (General Winthrop)
M. Emmet Walsh (Aide)
Roy E. Glenn, Sr. (Lawyer)
Peter Forster (Cardinal)
Norman Burton (Army Officer)
William Woodson (Naval Officer)
Tom Lowell (Orderly)
Gene Whittington (Marine Captain)
Donald Elson (Curator)
Bill Bonds (TV Newscaster)
Army Archerd (Referee)
James Bacon (General Faulkner)
Ricardo Montalban (Armando)
John Alderman (Corporal)
Steve Roberts (General Brody)
Jack Berle (U.S. Secretary of State)

REVIEWS:

"I cannot think of any fantasy film series that has evolved as dynamically or as inventively as these three films while maintaining so convincingly a continuous and consistent storyline." (*Cinefantastique*)

". . . a hairy fairy tale lacking in imagination and abounding in unintentional laughs. . . . Director Don Taylor mixes silliness with what will look like profound tragedy only to those who have never seen a movie." (*Cue*)

"*Escape from the Planet of the Apes* is an ingenious follow-up to its two predecessors. . . . A shrewd reworking — a mirror image of the original picture." (*Los Angeles Herald-Examiner*)

The best friend a chimp ever had: Bradford Dillman played Dr. Lewis Dixon in *Escape from the Planet of the Apes* (Globe Photos).

"Nobody is going to believe it, but I must say anyway that Don Taylor's *Escape from the Planet of the Apes* is one of the better new movies in town." (*New York Times*)

"*Escape from the Planet of the Apes* is an excellent film. Far better than last year's follow-up and almost as good as the original *Planet of the Apes*. May this series continue as an annual summer event." (*Variety*)

THE BALANCE SHEET:
Escape from the Planet of the Apes was made for $2.5 million; the film ranked #17 on *Variety*'s box-office chart for 1971, earning $5.5 million in its original release.

WHAT IT'S ABOUT:

The U.S. military rescues a strange aircraft from the ocean, and the soldiers are astonished when three spacesuit-garbed apes emerge from inside. The "ape-o-nauts," Cornelius, Zira, and Milo, are transferred to the Los Angeles Zoo infirmary for study by two scientists, Dr. Lewis Dixon and Dr. Stephanie Branton. When left alone, the apes conspire to hide their intelligence from the humans, and to not divulge that they've journeyed back in time 2,000 years. But after Milo is killed by a gorilla in the next cage, Cornelius and Zira introduce themselves to their caretakers.

At a press conference, the two apes charm government officials and the media. But one scientist, Dr. Otto Hasslein, discovers that apes will one day rule over humans, and expresses concern to the president, especially after Zira announces that she is pregnant. Hasslein advises that Cornelius and Zira be killed, in the hope of changing the future. Under further interrogation, and the use of sodium Pentothol, Zira reveals that, in her time, she performed medical experiments on humans, who were often hunted for sport. The government orders her baby destroyed, and Zira to be sterilized.

With the help of Lewis and Stephanie, the apes escape military custody, and are hidden by Armando, a kindly circus owner. Hasslein hunts them down and kills them, but not before Zira gives birth to a son.

THE QUOTABLE APES:

"I don't like bananas." (Zira)

"If I urge the destruction of these two apes am I defying God's will — or obeying it? Am I His enemy or His instrument?" (Dr. Otto Hasslein)

WHAT'S GREAT ABOUT IT:

🐒 The pre-credit sequence. After the grim denouement of *Beneath*, in which the earth and Charlton Heston were blown to bits, Paul Dehn's script for *Escape* wisely opted for a lighter tone, and the fun begins right away. When the apes first remove their space helmets, the reactions of the soldiers are played primarily for laughs. The jazzy Jerry Goldsmith score skips the ram's horn and somber strings of the previous films in exchange for a twangy guitar and a surf rock rhythm track.

🦧 Role reversal. Cornelius and Zira are subjected to the same condescending treatment that Taylor received in *Planet of the Apes*. The wonderful early scenes, in which the apes are given intelligence tests, and the distinguished Dr. Zira is asked to fit colored blocks together to earn a banana as a reward, are the first genuinely funny moments in the series. Zira's inability to keep silent in the face of such presumption is marvelously played by Kim Hunter.

🦧 The backstory. During their testimony before a panel of government officials, Cornelius and Zira reveal how apes began to acquire intelligence, how they were enslaved by humans, and how they ultimately rebelled, thus foreshadowing the stories of the next two films.

🦧 The apes meet the 20th century. The middle third of the film is the most delightful extended sequence in the *Planet of the Apes* series. Cornelius and Zira check into the Beverly Wilshire Hotel in Beverly Hills, where Zira experiences her first bubble bath. The couple tour Los Angeles, garbed in more fashionable clothes than they arrived in, and become overnight celebrities. It's too bad they didn't film a scene alluded to in the story, in which the two apes christen a new boat at Disneyland's jungle cruise.

🦧 Eric Braeden as the President's senior science advisor, Dr. Otto Hasslein. He's the bad guy, but like Dr. Zaius in the first film, he is motivated to violence out of a desire to preserve the superiority of his species, at any cost. His determination to kill Zira's baby recalls the old moral debate about whether it would have been

The behind-the-scenes photos and film footage shot by Roddy McDowall were used in the 1998 documentary *Behind the Planet of the Apes* (Globe Photos).

acceptable to murder Adolf Hitler when he was born, to prevent the genocide he would orchestrate as an adult. Even Hasslein isn't certain about the course he has chosen, and confesses his pangs of conscience to the President in a pivotal scene.

WHAT'S NOT SO GREAT:

🦍 Dr. Hasslein's goofy "Infinite Regression" theory, which purports to explain how the apes arrived from the future. It's the most off-the-wall scientific theory in a movie since Commander Eros explained Solaronite in *Plan 9 From Outer Space*. Even a smooth-talker like Eric Braeden can't convincingly sell this bag of goods.

🦍 The apes' escape from the military base. Movie buffs are familiar with scenes of heroes held captive in a supposedly secure facility, and their subsequent break-out by eluding one uniformed soldier. In *Escape*, Cornelius and Zira slip out of the army's grasp in a textbook example of this cinema cliché.

DID YOU KNOW?

🦍 *Escape* was originally titled *The Secret of the Planet of the Apes*.

🦍 Natalie Trundy returns as Dr. Stephanie Branton. We'll see her again in the final two series entries.

🦍 Norman Burton, who plays an army officer here, appeared as an ape in the original *Planet of the Apes* and also appears in two episodes of the *Apes* television series.

🦍 In the world of the apes, the use of the word "monkey" is an insult, according to Cornelius.

🦍 Eric Braeden has portrayed Victor Newman on the CBS soap opera *The Young and the Restless* since 1980.

The stars of *Escape from the Planet of the Apes*: Milo the chimp, Ricardo Montalban, Natalie Trundy, and Bradford Dillman (Globe Photos).

🐾 Jack Berle, who plays the U.S. Secretary of State, is the brother of comedian Milton Berle.

🐾 *Escape* was a box-office hit, despite being promoted by a lackluster ad campaign that featured the tag line, "First *Planet* . . .

Then *Beneath* . . . Now the Hairiest of All!" Fox's publicity department urged theaters to forge promotional partnerships with local zoos and pet shops.

🦧 When scenes were shot in and around the Beverly Wilshire Hotel in Los Angeles, one motorist was so shocked by the sight of apes on Wilshire Boulevard that he plowed into three parked cars. "Every now and then we'd tease people in other cars, and wave at them as we drove by," said Kim Hunter, who was happy to reprise her role as Zira one more time. "I adored the script," she raved.

🦧 Zira's 20th century fashions were designed by Giorgio's Dress Shop; Cornelius's suit was purchased from Dick Carroll's Men's Shop.

🦧 Armando's Circus was set up on a golf course across the street from Twentieth Century Fox.

CONQUEST OF THE PLANET OF THE APES
(Twentieth Century Fox, 1972)
Directed by J. Lee Thompson; Written by Paul Dehn; Produced by Arthur P. Jacobs; Photographed by Bruce Surtees; Edited by Marjorie Fowler and Alan Jaggs; Music by Tom Scott; Art direction by Philip Jeffries; Set decoration by Norman Rockett; Makeup by Joe DiBella and Jack Barron, supervised by Dan Striepeke.

CAST:
Roddy McDowall (Caesar)
Don Murray (Breck)
Ricardo Montalban (Armando)
Natalie Trundy (Lisa)
Hari Rhodes (MacDonald)

Severn Darden (Kolp)
Lou Wagner (Busboy)
John Randolph (Commission Chairman)
Asa Maynor (Mrs. Riley)
H.M. Wynant (Hoskyns)
David Chow (Aldo)
Buck Kartalian (Frank)
John Dennis (Policeman)
Gordon Jump (Auctioneer)
Dick Spangler (Announcer)
Joyce Haber (Zelda)
Hector Soucy (Ape with Chain)
Paul Comi (Policeman #2)

REVIEWS:

"My favorite of the lot. While the ending is a bit preachy, this version is fluidly and inventively directed by J. Lee Thompson. The story unfolds with clarity and the cutesy elements are gone." (*Cue*)

"Another exciting adventure story, which somehow manages to care fairly deeply about man's inhumanity to man, and it is all acceptable because in this case man is ape and a chimpanzee can get away with any amount of moralising because the sermon comes in such an unusual form." (*Films and Filming*)

"Round Four. Not quite a knockout, but a solid win. Starts in fine. Lots of action. Few neat quick jabs to the morals. Fair dose of spectacle. Toward the end the nifty footwork gets a little tired and too much philosophical chat bogs down the pace." (*Los Angeles Herald-Examiner*)

"That *Conquest of the Planet of the Apes* is actually the fourth in the series is awe-inspiring, for the films on the whole have been remarkably consistent in quality. Indeed, No. 4 may well be the best since *Planet of the Apes*." (*Los Angeles Times*)

"It's not bad. . . . Wait till you see the last battle royal! [The] audience cheered the persevering apes and so did I. At 'em, boys!" (*New York Times*)

"*Conquest of the Planet of the Apes* is the handsomest of the lot. It has the same storybook gusto and bizarre pageantry as the original." (*Time*)

"The *Planet of the Apes* feature film series, perhaps the most successful ever to blend intelligent and thought-provoking story matter with broad entertainment values, takes an angry turn in the fourth entry. Handsomely produced . . . deftly directed . . . and well-written." (*Variety*)

THE BALANCE SHEET:

Conquest of the Planet of the Apes was made for $1.7 million; the film ranked #28 on *Variety*'s box-office chart for 1972, earning $4.5 million in its original release.

WHAT IT'S ABOUT:

As Cornelius had foretold before his death, apes have become slaves to humans by the year 1991. Caesar, the child of Cornelius, has grown to maturity under the guidance of his surrogate father, Armando. During a visit to Los Angeles to promote Armando's circus, Caesar witnesses an ape being beaten by police, and cannot resist voicing his outrage. In the ensuing melee Armando is detained by the authorities; Caesar manages to escape. He removes his garments to blend in with a new shipment of apes just arrived from Africa.

The apes are brutalized into learning menial tasks. Though he keeps silent, Caesar unintentionally displays his superior intelligence, and falls under the suspicion of Governor Breck. Having learned of Armando's connection to Cornelius and Zira, Breck suspects that Caesar may be the slain couple's son, long believed dead. He buys Caesar at a slave auction.

Don Murray portrayed the villainous Governor Breck in *Conquest of the Planet of the Apes* (Globe Photos).

Armando is interrogated by the government but refuses to reveal any information about Caesar. He is killed while trying to escape. Caesar begins to covertly organize a resistance movement among the apes, until his identity is discovered. MacDonald, a government official sympathetic to the apes' cause, helps Caesar to escape and joins the uprising. Led by Caesar, the apes soon gain control of the city, and apprehend Breck and his staff. Caesar vows revenge on the humans, but ultimately chooses to show mercy on his former captors. History, he observes, is on the side of the apes.

THE QUOTABLE APES:

"When we hate you, we're hating the dark side of ourselves."
(Breck, to Caesar)

"We who are not human can afford to be humane." (Caesar)

"Tonight we have seen the birth of the planet of the apes!" (Caesar)

WHAT'S GREAT ABOUT IT:

The allegorical condemnation of slavery in 18th and 19th century America. The futuristic story teaches a harsh lesson about the past; Paul Dehn's script clearly draws a parallel between apes in 1991 and African-Americans in 1791. Both were shipped from Africa against their will, sold at auction, ill-treated by their "masters," and had no rights under the law. It is fitting that MacDonald, an African-American and the governor's second-in-command, would come to Caesar's aid.

Caesar's reaction to the news of Armando's death, when his devastation slowly turns to anger. The change registers clearly on the face of Roddy McDowall who, beneath layers of latex, uses his eyes as the windows of Caesar's soul. Caesar's speech to his army of apes after the climactic battle is another revelation. In the first draft of the script, the speech was even more militant, and Caesar did not reconsider his original verdict on Breck and those responsible for his enslavement. A more benevolent ending was added in post-production; no new scenes were filmed, but new dialogue is spoken over close-ups of Caesar, Lisa, and MacDonald.

The triumph of the military-industrial complex. It's amazing how many science fiction projects envisioned our planet's future the way it appears in *Conquest*: buildings of glass and steel, basic black the primary color of fashion and interior design, civil and military authority represented by a modern day Gestapo, and a lazy populace engaged only in the pursuit of pleasure, and apathetic to its consequences.

🐒 Natalie Trundy, having already played a telepathic mutant in *Beneath* and a human scientist in *Escape*, now changes species to portray Caesar's girlfriend, Lisa. She would reprise the character in the fifth and final film.

WHAT'S NOT SO GREAT:
🐒 If everyone was paying attention to Cornelius and Zira, and knew that the ascension of the apes would begin with their enslavement, wouldn't someone in authority make an effort to not go down that road?

🐒 Humans resorting to the enslavement of another species just to solve a busboy shortage seems like a pretty strained premise. Even if we accept that people gradually transformed their pet apes into employees and domestics, it's obvious that the creatures never really get the hang of it. The cost of replacement glassware alone would have squelched the idea pretty quick. And where was PETA when all this was happening?

🐒 The torture of Caesar. Despite disturbing scenes of violence in all five *Apes* films, including the murders of Cornelius and Zira in *Escape* and the destruction of an entire planet in *Beneath*, *Conquest* is the only film in the series to receive a 'PG' (as opposed to 'G') rating. The ape uprising is partly responsible, comprising the final third of the film and racking up a *Die Hard*-worthy body count. But far more harrowing is the scene in which Caesar is strapped to a metal table by Breck's soldiers and tortured into confessing his identity. As his body contorts in agony and his screams echo down the sterile metallic corridors, Caesar finally breaks, and whimpers for mercy. It's the most unsettling moment in the series.

🐒 Don Murray's grandiose performance as Governor Breck, who

comes off so smarmy that it's hard to believe he could ever be elected to public office. Humanity is pretty screwed up in this version of our future, but even Americans who would hire apes to style hair and serve drinks should still see through a politician that's this seedy and corrupt.

DID YOU KNOW?

🐒 Most of the film was shot in Los Angeles at Century City and the University of California, at Irvine. Century City, a commercial/ office complex in Beverly Hills, still looks much the same as it did in 1972. Sharp-eyed viewers will have no problem finding the backdrops used for several skirmishes between apes and soldiers.

🐒 In keeping with the films' themes of prejudice and class warfare, the riot scenes were modeled after the actual riots that occurred in Watts, California, in 1965.

🐒 At test screenings in Phoenix and Las Vegas, the same cities where the previous series' entries were tested, *Conquest* received a grade of "excellent" from 92 percent of the audience, the highest scores tallied for any *Planet of the Apes* film.

🐒 Mervyn LeRoy, director of such movie classics as *Blossoms in the Dust* (1941), *Little Caesar* (1930), and *Mr. Roberts* (1955), plays a chimpanzee during the final battle scene.

🐒 Producer Arthur Jacobs offered bit parts in all of the *Apes* films to members of the press, in an effort to court free publicity. *Los Angeles Herald-Examiner* columnist James Bacon was one of Jacobs' most enthusiastic extras; he played a gorilla in the first two series entries, and appears in the first scene of *Escape* as a four-star General. In *Conquest*, Bacon's high hopes for further promotion were dashed when he was busted back to playing an ape in a crowd scene. Bacon is the only person to appear in all five *Planet of the Apes* movies.

BATTLE FOR THE PLANET OF THE APES
(Twentieth Century Fox, 1973)

Directed by J. Lee Thompson; Written by John William Corrington and Joyce Hooper Corrington, based on a story by Paul Dehn; Produced by Arthur P. Jacobs; Photographed by Richard H. Kline; Edited by Alan L. Jaggs and John C. Horger; Music by Leonard Rosenman; Makeup by Jack Barron and Werner Keppler, supervised by Joe DiBella.

CAST:

Roddy McDowall (Caesar)
Claude Akins (Aldo)
John Huston (Lawgiver)
Natalie Trundy (Lisa)
Severn Darden (Kolp)
Lew Ayres (Mandemus)
Paul Williams (Virgil)
Austin Stoker (MacDonald)
Noah Keen (Teacher)
Richard Eastham (Mutant Captain)
France Nuyen (Alma)
Paul Stevens (Mendez)
Heather Lowe (Doctor)
Bobby Porter (Cornelius)
Michael Stearns (Jake)
Cal Wilson (Soldier)
Pat Cardi (Young Chimp)
John Landis (Jake's Friend)
Andy Knight (Mutant on Motorcycle)

REVIEWS

". . . suffering from acute screenplay strain." (*Cue*)

"Like the other movies, *Battle* is both wonderful entertainment and a politically sophisticated fable, a chance for children to learn about the forces that move the world in a way that's accessible and imaginative." (*Hollywood Reporter*)

"While the premise . . . might seem slightly contrived, it is a fun movie with action, wit, and fine acting." (*Los Angeles Herald-Examiner*)

"Although *Battle for the Planet of the Apes* is launched from a more thinly contrived premise than any of its predecessors it becomes just as involving as they were, thanks to the strong appeal of the series' allegorical underpinnings and to the adroit direction of J. Lee Thompson." (*Los Angeles Times*)

"Still unamusing except for the masks, but it's passable small kids' stuff." (*New Republic*)

"*Battle for the Planet of the Apes* is not great, but it is appealing and a bit sad. . . . The chimpanzee and orangutan makeup remains remarkable, and the lines are occasionally bright and funny. There are far worse ways of wasting time." (*New York Times*)

"It's not so much that this final effort is limp, but that the previous four pix maintained for so long a good quality level. . . . *Apes* was a great film series until everyone got tired." (*Variety*)

"Now the fourth sequel in the series, *Battle for the Planet of the Apes* ends it all with more of a thud than a bang — prolonging the concept but, again, failing to extend the idea." (*Washington Post*)

THE BALANCE SHEET:

Battle for the Planet of the Apes was made for $1.8 million; the film ranked #31 on *Variety*'s box-office chart for 1973, earning $4 million in its original release.

WHAT IT'S ABOUT:

In 2670 AD, a teacher relates the story of Caesar, the legendary ape who led his species out of captivity. Ten years after apes first cast off their chains, a great world war reduced major cities to rubble. Human beings regressed to a state of primitive society, and apes asserted their dominance over what remained of life on earth. Caesar leads one settlement, in which apes and men live together in harmony, though it is clear that men are now subservient to their simian brethren. General Aldo, an ambitious gorilla, urges Caesar to clarify the superior status of the ape.

When Caesar begins to question his method of leadership, his friend MacDonald suggests that he visit the ruins of the forbidden city, where videotapes of Cornelius and Zira may still exist to offer guidance. Once in the city, Caesar and his party encounter a colony of hostile, mutated humans, and narrowly avoid capture.

Caesar's son, Cornelius, overhears Aldo's plan to launch a military coup. His presence is discovered and Cornelius falls from a tree while attempting to flee. Caesar refuses to leave the bedside of his gravely injured son. In the interim, while the mutants prepare to invade the ape colony, Aldo seizes power and orders all humans imprisoned.

The mutants are defeated in battle. A dispute between Caesar and Aldo over control of the ape colony is resolved after Aldo's role in the death of Cornelius is revealed.

THE QUOTABLE APES:

"Every Caesar must have his Brutus." (Governor Kolp)

WHAT'S GREAT ABOUT IT:

🐵 Caesar as messiah. The story of Cornelius, Zira, and Caesar, reprised through flashbacks to *Escape* and *Conquest,* has taken on biblical significance in Ape history. Caesar's birth, like that of Christ, symbolizes the arrival of a savior for his people, though there are also traces of the Moses story in Caesar's leading his

Claude Akins played the evil General Aldo in *Battle for the Planet of the Apes* (Y. Kahana/ Shooting Star).

people out of captivity. It is fitting, then, that the film opens hundreds of years after Caesar's death, with a scene of his legend being taught to a new generation.

John Huston as the Lawgiver. *Battle* suffers a loss of dignity in other aspects compared to its series' predecessors, but some of that dignity is restored by Huston's monologues, which open and close the film. Why would one of Hollywood's most revered directors (*The Maltese Falcon, The African Queen*, and too many more to list) sit through three hours of makeup to play an orangutan for less than five minutes on screen? Huston offers no explanation in his autobiography, *An Open Book*, but other biographers have suggested he took the role to pick up extra money for his weekly Friday night poker game.

🐒 The gorilla soldiers. We haven't seen the bellicose black-clad warriors riding their ebony horses since *Beneath the Planet of the Apes,* and their nasty-as-they-wanna-be presence was missed. Claude Akins makes an effective gorilla leader. He'd later draw upon his simian experience when playing opposite a chimpanzee named Bear in the television series *B.J. and the Bear.*

🐒 The supporting performances of Natalie Trundy, who gets to speak in this film as Caesar's wife, Lisa; singer/composer Paul Williams as the ape planet's shortest orangutan; and Austin Stoker as the brother of the government official who helped Caesar in *Conquest.*

🐒 The mutant convoy, driving across a post-apocalyptic landscape in patched-together vehicles, might have inspired similar scenes in George Miller's *The Road Warrior* (1981).

WHAT'S NOT SO GREAT:

🐒 Diminishing returns. *Battle* is the most disappointing entry in the series, and a less than satisfying conclusion to the cinematic chapter of this epic science fiction saga. From the abysmal dialogue ("Let us reason together — and make plans") to the cringe-worthy final shot of the crying Caesar statue, the movie barely rises above Golden Turkey status. It's tempting to blame the loss of writer Paul Dehn, who died before production began. But Dehn's finished story treatment had already been rejected. Producers wanted something a little more upbeat after the dark tone of *Conquest,* and turned to writers John William Corrington and Joyce Wilson Corrington, who had a sci-fi hit with the Charlton Heston film *The Omega Man* (1971). The Corringtons just didn't have the same deft touch with the material that Dehn showed in the three previous entries.

🐒 Filling time. Even at just 86 minutes, *Battle* seems padded to reach feature-length, first with extended flashbacks to previous films in the series, and then with small-scale battle scenes that, unlike those in *Conquest,* do not generate much excitement. Caesar's return to the city contains a lot of stealthy corridor-walking, reminiscent of old *Dr. Who* episodes, in which the characters wander in circles through the various spaceships of the week.

🐒 Did I mention the crying statue of Caesar?

DID YOU KNOW?

🐒 Lew Ayres (Mandemus) appeared in several motion picture classics, dating back to 1930's *All Quiet on the Western Front.* From 1938 to 1942, he played Dr. Kildare in a series of popular medical dramas.

🐒 John Landis, a former stuntman and part-time actor who would later direct the comedies *Animal House* (1978) and *The Blues Brothers* (1980), plays Jake's friend.

🐒 When director J. Lee Thompson heard that the Ape City set was being surveyed by Twentieth Century Fox for possible use in a *Planet of the Apes* television series, he quipped, "I wonder if they'll want it when I get through with it." He then blew up the whole set during *Battle*'s explosive climax.

🐒 Paul Williams, an Academy Award-winning songwriter (for "Evergreen" from *A Star is Born*), was offered the role of Virgil after an appearance on *The Tonight Show* with Johnny Carson. Casting director Ross Brown thought he had an interesting presence, and invited him to audition for the role.

🐒 The role of the Lawgiver was originally offered to actor Sam Jaffe, but he turned it down, refusing to shave his beard for the makeup and facial appliances.

🐾 The original script for *Battle* contained more overt references to the Alpha-Omega bomb, which caused the destruction of the planet in *Beneath the Planet of the Apes*, and ties the continuity of the films more closely together. These references were omitted in subsequent drafts, but revived by writer Doug Moench in his comic book adaptation of the films.

🐾 Twentieth Century Fox shifted their publicity department into overdrive on behalf of *Battle for the Planet of the Apes*. Press kits were sent to movie theaters with a variety of suggestions for drumming up business. Among the more bizarre:

> "Stage a contest to find the 'Most Beautiful Gorill(a) in the World.' The girl contestants wear bathing suits, bikinis, hot pants, etc., but they must put on an ape mask to be judged."

> "Organize a girl ape and boy ape baseball team calling itself 'The Ape Planets.' Outfit the girls and boys in ape masks. Have them challenge other ballplayers to softball matches."

> "Engage a gymnastic boy and girl dressed scantily, wearing ape masks, to perform acrobatics at your theater. If there is some way to utilize the area above your marquee, so much the better."

CHAPTER THREE

APES ON TELEVISION

PLANET OF THE APES: THE TELEVISION SERIES

In September 1973, CBS paid $1 million for the first broadcast rights to *Planet of the Apes*. As *Austin Powers*'s Dr. Evil might say, one million dollars is a lot of money, especially back in 1973. But it turned out to be well spent; network executives were shocked when the movie drew a phenomenal 60 share in the ratings. That means more than one-half of all television sets in use that night were tuned in to the adventures of Taylor, Cornelius, and Zira.

CBS programmers wondered if the appeal of the films could be recaptured in a *Planet of the Apes* television series. It wasn't a new idea; producer Arthur Jacobs considered proposing a series one year earlier, but opted instead to return to the big screen for the fifth time with *Battle For the Planet of the Apes*. But when *Battle* opened to mixed reviews and lower box-office returns, Jacobs was convinced that any further adventures belonged on television. Sadly, just as he began preparing an outline for the series, he died of a heart attack in 1973.

The production chores were taken over by writers Art Wallace and Anthony Wilson, both experts at launching new shows. Art Wallace worked with producer Dan Curtis to create the phenomenally successful gothic daytime drama, *Dark Shadows* (1966–71). Wilson worked on the popular Western series *Lancer* (1968–71),

"ANSA" astronauts Pete Burke (James Naughton, left) and Alan Virdon (Ron Harper) prepare to blast off in the *Planet of the Apes* television series (Globe Photos).

and the NBC Mystery Movies featuring George Peppard as Banacek. They were joined by story consultants Joe Ruby and Ken Spears, best known for their work on the great, goofy Sid & Marty Krofft shows that made Saturday mornings in the 1970s so much fun. Ruby and Spears created *Wonderbug, Magic Mongo,* and *ElectraWoman and DynaGirl.* Several Krofft show veterans would make guest appearances on the *Apes* series, including Jay Robinson (*Dr. Shrinker*) and Norman Alden (*ElectraWoman*).

Wallace and Wilson went back to the first *Planet of the Apes* film for their concept, hoping to recapture the same sense of wonder that audiences experienced in 1967. In the pilot, two astronauts, Alan Virdon and Pete Burke, crash-land on earth in the distant future. They soon discover that their planet is now under the rule of intelligent apes, who look down upon humans as an inferior but dangerous species. The astronauts' ongoing efforts to find a way back to their own time, while staying one step ahead of the gorilla soldiers led by General Urko, offered abundant opportunities for adventure.

The television series would not embrace the cynical, misanthropic tone of the movies. Though episodes such as "The Legacy" acknowledge that man destroyed his own civilization, it was not something that Burke and Virdon agonized over, the way Taylor and Brent did in the first two films. However, Art Wallace still saw the potential to use the futuristic scenario to comment on contemporary society. "We were particularly concerned with commenting on racial violence," Wallace said. "The apes were dealt with as if they were another race, separate but equal. The idea was that it was the white man getting stepped on."

Roddy McDowall was approached to appear in the series and, somewhat to the producers' surprise, he eagerly signed on to create yet another ape character. He played Galen, a genial, inquisitive chimpanzee who would join Burke and Virdon on their journeys. "All the attributes of Galen were ones as a human being I would be happy to embrace and only wish I could [possess], so it was a wonderful skin to be inside," McDowall told the

Sci-Fi Channel. "I adored playing him because he was so full of fun." Though the actor is still more associated with Cornelius and Caesar, he confessed that of all his ape portrayals, "I liked Galen the best."

The role of Alan Virdon went to Ron Harper, a veteran of several short-lived TV series. Harper had played a police detective in *87th Precinct* (1961–62), a World War II commando in *Garrison's Gorillas* (1967–68), and comedic roles in such forgotten shows as *The Jean Arthur Show* and *Wendy and Me*. *Planet of the Apes* was his fifth attempt at a hit show, and he was confident that he had found a winner at last.

Before being cast as Pete Burke, James Naughton's only television credit was as the estranged son of a detective played by Dan Dailey in *Faraday and Company* (1973–74). Prior to that, he had played one of John Houseman's students in the hit film *The Paper Chase* (1973).

Booth Colman played Dr. Zaius, the only character from the films to appear in the television series. Colman studied ape behavior at the zoo to prepare for the role. He wore the same costume that Maurice Evans had worn in the first two films, which had been preserved at the Fox studio. "I found an old British lotto ticket in an inside pocket and returned it to Maurice by mail," said Colman in a 1992 interview. "He wrote back, wishing me luck with the series and hoping that they had washed and ironed everything for me!"

General Urko, the astronauts' chief adversary, was played by Mark Lenard as a simian Lt. Gerard, always one step behind his fugitives. Lenard's fiery portrayal of the passionate, hate-consumed Urko could not be further removed from his other prominent sci-fi creation: the cool, logic-driven Sarek, the father of *Star Trek*'s Mr. Spock.

As filming commenced in the summer of 1974, all the elements seemed to be in place for an entertaining show. Lalo Schifrin, best known for his theme from *Mission: Impossible*, created a suitable opening fanfare complete with ram's horn, reminiscent of Jerry Goldsmith's movie score. The terrific opening titles sequence is still fondly recalled by fans. Next to the Statue of Liberty revelation at the end of the first film, the most memorable image in the *Planet of the Apes* mythos might be the sequence's final shot of the gorilla soldiers on horseback, rifles raised overhead, silhouetted in a burning yellow-orange sunset.

Makeup artist Dan Striepeke, who worked with John Chambers on the *Apes* films, recreated the movies' trademark ape appliances for the series. Roddy McDowall spent more than three hours in the makeup chair every day to transform into Galen, but after a few episodes, Ron Harper once recalled that McDowall's face "looked like raw hamburger" from wearing the rubber appliances for 12 hours at a stretch. He had to take a week off for his skin to heal.

The makeup caused other problems as well. In the summer of 1974, temperatures at the Twentieth Century Fox ranch in Malibu, California, topped 100 degrees; actors and stuntmen garbed in heavy gorilla soldier uniforms, their heads completely enclosed in hair, rubber and glue, routinely collapsed from the heat. Bill Derwin, an assistant director, called *Planet of the Apes* "physically the toughest TV series ever made."

As the fall TV season approached, advance word on *Planet of the Apes* was encouraging. CBS programmer Fred Silverman hailed the pilot as "The best first episode of a TV series I've ever seen," and industry analysts such as *TV Guide* were certain the show couldn't miss. Originally scheduled to air Tuesday evenings, the series was moved to Fridays at 8 p.m. The premiere earned an impressive 34 share, but still trailed the 46 share garnered by NBC's *Sanford and Son* and *Chico and the Man.* ABC's popular action series *The Six Million Dollar Man*, which aired Fridays at 8:30, also cut into the new show's audience.

Negative reviews didn't help. "The premiere episode contained not a trace of political or sociological significance — no satire, chilling or otherwise," wrote *Variety.* "And the ape makeup and costuming that gulled movie audiences was only ludicrous in this retarded excuse in action-adventure television." When the ratings didn't pick up, CBS chose to cancel the series before the end of its first season.

No one can say for certain why *Planet of the Apes* did not enjoy a more successful run on television. It was the second most popular show with the 2–11 age group, but never captured the imagination of teenagers and older viewers. "Of people 50 and over, apparently only four are watching," Fred Silverman told *TV Guide*. "Two old ladies in Iowa and a couple who owns a zoo."

The series never developed a consistent tone. Its fourteen episodes were divided almost equally between action-themed stories ("The Gladiators," "Tomorrow's Tide"), and humanistic tales that focused on social issues ("The Good Seeds," "The Surgeon"). Unfortunately, the action stories that appealed most to the series' biggest audience quickly fell into an all-too-familiar pattern; Burke, Virdon, or Galen would be captured, and the others would ride to the rescue.

Surprisingly, the series found a much more enthusiastic audience in England as well as other markets around the world, with one notable exception; Indonesian viewers criticized the series, saying it was "unbelievable that man could fall under apes' orders."

But as the *Planet of the Apes* phenomenon continued throughout the ensuing decades, the series enjoyed a renewed popularity among fans. James Naughton revealed in the documentary *Behind the Planet of the Apes* that he still gets fan mail from his days as Pete Burke. When Ron Harper was invited to host a telethon in Sydney, Australia, he was teamed with former "Monkee" Micky Dolenz. When he arrived at the Sydney airport, he was greeted by a guy dressed like an ape.

In 1980, the Sci-Fi channel aired all fourteen episodes, including "The Liberator," which was never originally broadcast on CBS. The series was also re-edited into five two-hour TV movies, for syndication by Fox in 1981. The movies still turn up on TBS from time to time. *Back to the Planet of the Apes* combines "Escape from Tomorrow" and "The Trap"; *Forgotten City of the*

Planet of the Apes combines "The Gladiators" and "The Legacy"; *Treachery and Greed on the Planet of the Apes* combines "The Horse Race" and "The Tyrant"; *Life, Liberty and Pursuit of the Planet of the Apes* combines "The Surgeon" and "The Interrogation"; and *Farewell to the Planet of the Apes* combines "Tomorrow's Tide" and "Up Above the World So High."

PLANET OF THE APES
CBS, Fridays, 8 p.m.–9 p.m.
September 13, 1974–December 27, 1974

EPISODE GUIDE
Cast:
Ron Harper (Alan Virdon)
James Naughton (Pete Burke)
Roddy McDowall (Galen)
Booth Colman (Dr. Zaius)
Mark Lenard (Urko)

EPISODE ONE: ESCAPE FROM TOMORROW
Original Airdate: September 13, 1974
Produced by: Stan Hough
Written by: Art Wallace
Directed by: Don Weis

Guest Stars: Royal Dano (Farrow), Woodrow Parfrey (Veska), Biff Elliot (Ullman), Bobby Porter (Arno), Jerome Thor (Proto), William Beckley (Grundig), Alvin Hammer (Man).

After a turbulent space flight, astronauts Alan Virdon and Pete Burke pass through a bend in time, and crash-land on earth in the year 3085. They are astonished to discover that, 2000 years into the future, the world is ruled by intelligent apes, and man has been reduced to a primitive state.

The astronauts are captured and put on trial in Central City, where their fate is debated by the ruling elders. Galen, a chimpanzee, discovers how intelligent the two prisoners are, and questions the lessons he was taught about human history. Dr. Zaius, head of the science council, warns Galen against further investigation. But when Galen overhears the malevolent General Urko planning to kill Burke and Virdon, he saves their lives. The astronauts return the favor by breaking Galen out of prison, after he is jailed for heresy. Branded as outlaws, the three new friends join forces. Before escaping from Central City, Virdon finds a computer disk from their spacecraft that might provide information on how the astronauts can return to their own time.

Commentary

The five *Planet of the Apes* films followed a story arc that began in the distant future, jumped back to the present day, and ended somewhere in between. The television series is set back on the planet as seen in the first film, with its Gaudi-esque ape settlement, gorilla soldiers, and orangutan historical revisionists. But the time is different, nearly 900 years before Taylor bellowed "Get your stinking paws off me" according to Art Wallace's script. Burke and Virdon meet humans that are more advanced than the mute tribe dressed in animal skins that Taylor and Brent encountered; they have villages of their own, and work as farmers and laborers.

Technically, Burke and Virdon are the first pilots to crash on the ape planet (in 3085 according to their onboard computer), and the first to meet Dr. Zaius, who must take very good care of himself if he was still around to greet Taylor in 3955. Booth Colman plays the learned doctor, and never strays very far from the template established in the films by Maurice Evans.

There's a relaxed, natural camaraderie between stars Ron Harper and James Naughton, though a bit more conflict between the characters might have added another dimension to their friendship — nothing serious, just minor personality clashes played for humor or drama, as often seen in other "buddy" shows like *Starsky and Hutch*. One senses that both actors could have brought much more to their roles and their on-screen relationship if they were ever asked to do so in the material they played.

Roddy McDowall's Galen is a different character from Cornelius and Caesar, despite the inevitable physical resemblance. The gentle, erudite but somewhat naïve Galen is not as quick to anger as Cornelius, nor does he have the military acumen of Caesar. And of all McDowall's simian altar-egos, Galen has the best sense of humor, and offers the actor his best opportunity to show a lighter side in the mythos.

The computer disk is introduced as a method for one day returning the astronauts to the 1980s, and one assumes that if the series had continued this plot thread might have been further developed. As it is, the disk is mentioned in only two more episodes.

EPISODE TWO: THE GLADIATORS

Original Airdate: September 20, 1974
Produced by: Stan Hough
Written by: Art Wallace
Directed by: Don McDougall

Guest Stars: William Smith (Tolar), John Hoyt (Barlow), Marc Singer (Dalton), Pat Renella (Jason), Andy Albin (Man), Eddie Fontaine (Gorilla Sergeant), Nick Dimitri (Gorilla), Ron Stein (1st Gorilla), Jim Stader (2nd Gorilla).

Barlow, a village prefect, believes the best way for humans to work out their innate aggression is to pit them against each other in combat to the death. While Galen tries to explain to the prefect the inhumanity of his village's most popular spectator sport, Burke is captured and forced to compete against Tolar, an undefeated champion.

Commentary

The show is a rather simplistic adaptation on the gladiator games of ancient Rome. Prefect Barlow justifies the practice as necessary to keep men docile, so they won't start killing each other outside the arena, and take the rest of the planet with them like they did once before. Though Barlow seems more sympathetic to humans than most apes in authority, there is some question as to whether he created the games as sound public policy, or for his own amusement.

The actual fight between Burke and Tolar, however, is more overstaged than a midcard match in the World Wrestling Federation. William Smith seems to be channeling Jack Palance in his grandiose performance as the proud gladiator.

One of the most intriguing ongoing themes in the series is captivity, as both a mental and physical condition. The captive mindset is manifested here by Tolar, who is reprieved from a death sentence after losing in the arena, but feels outrage toward Burke instead of gratitude. In several episodes, the two astronauts open doors — material and symbolic — for oppressed villagers, but the people of earth's future are wary of the prospect of freedom.

Marc Singer plays Dalton, son of the disgraced gladiator Tolar. Singer would return to sword and sandal adventure in *The Beastmaster* (1982), a cult movie that still airs on television almost once a week.

EPISODE THREE: THE TRAP

Original Airdate: September 27, 1974
Produced by: Stan Hough
Written by: Edward J. Lakso
Directed by: Arnold Laven

Guest Stars: Norman Alden (Zako), John Milford (Miller), Cindy Eilbacher (Lisa Miller), Mickey LeClair (Jick Miller), Wallace Earl (Mary Miller), Gail Bonney (Old Woman).

After playing Sarek on *Star Trek*, Mark Lenard donned battle armor as General Urko, nemesis to Burke and Virdon (Globe Photos).

In a small farming village, Burke and Virdon find parts from a 21st-century computer. They trace the parts back to what's left of the city of San Francisco, with General Urko and his men in hot pursuit.

During an earthquake, Burke and Urko are separated from their allies when they fall through a fissure and into the ruins of a subway station. The two enemies are forced to work together if they are to have any chance of escape. On the surface, Virdon and Galen also join forces with Urko's troops to help their friends; but the alliances are threatened when Urko sees a poster for the San Francisco Zoo, depicting an ape in a cage.

Commentary

In this and subsequent episodes, it is established that the astronauts crash-landed on the West coast of the United States, unlike Taylor and Brent in the first two films, who found themselves in what used to be New York City. But all our space program castaways get chased by the bicoastal Dr. Zaius, who clearly gets around.

"The Trap" was written by Edward Lakso, a veteran television screenwriter whose name can be found in the credits of dozens of different TV shows, including half the 109 episodes of *Charlie's Angels*. In this pivotal episode, General Urko first learns of the human civilization that preceded his own, and finds the idea of subservient apes difficult to accept.

As Urko's sidekick, Zako, Norman Alden has one of those voices that is instantly familiar to anyone who watched television in the 1970s.

EPISODE FOUR: THE GOOD SEEDS
Original Airdate: October 4, 1974
Produced by: Stan Hough
Written by: Robert W. Lenski
Directed by: Don Weis

Guest Stars: Geoffrey Deuel (Anto), Lonny Chapman (Polar),

Jacqueline Scott (Zantes), Bobby Porter (Remus), Eileen Dietz Elber (Jillia), John Garwood (Police Gorilla), Dennis Cross (Gorilla Officer), Michael Carr (Patrol Rider), Fred Lerner (Police Gorilla).

Burke and Virdon carry an injured Galen into an ape village for medical treatment. The suspicious locals dislike having humans around, but agree to hide them from Urko's soldiers. The astronauts amaze area farmers by showing them advanced farming techniques, such as the use of a windmill, but one superstitious young ape, Anto, refuses to trust them, believing that humans bring bad luck. He vows to kill the two men if his pregnant cow is "cursed," and doesn't give birth to a male calf.

Commentary

An excellent episode that focuses on the alliance between the astronauts and a humble family of ape farmers, who greet the human fugitives with varying degrees of tolerance. When the series emphasized characters and relationships over action, the results were usually more satisfying. We get more insight into ape culture, particularly their superstitions. According to Anto, it is bad luck for humans to sleep near a cow.

Details of the astronauts' backgrounds are also revealed here; Pete Burke expresses regret over not buying a bar in his hometown of Jersey City, while Alan Virdon recalls his life on a farm in Jackson County. The episode's best moment has Virdon explaining the best way to plant seeds to the apes' young son, Remus. That Alan could recall his own son in this child of another species is one of the episode's more subtly-expressed messages.

EPISODE FIVE: THE LEGACY
Original Airdate: October 11, 1974
Produced by: Stan Hough
Written by: Robert Hamner
Directed by: Bernard McEveety

Guest Stars: Zina Bethune (Arn), Jackie Earle Haley (Kraik), Robert Phillips (Gorilla Captain), Jon Lormer (Scientist), Wayne Foster (Gorilla Sergeant), Victor Killian (Human).

In the ruins of Oakland, California, Burke and Virdon wander through what's left of a building that used to house a government think-tank. Inside a vacuum-sealed vault, they find a recorded message left by scientists, who knew the destruction of human society was imminent. The recording reveals that a nearby underground storage facility contains computer records of the sum and substance of all human knowledge. The astronauts hope to find something that will help them return to their own time. But before they can investigate, Virdon is captured. While he bonds with a young woman and her son, who have also been imprisoned by the apes, Burke and Galen try to rescue their friend without being apprehended by Dr. Zaius.

Commentary

It's always amusing to see how production designers in the 1970s envisioned the super computers of the future. There's not an iMac in sight in the government facility as depicted here; instead, it's the standard issue floor models with the banks of flashing lights and spinning tape reels. The Robinson family had the same machines on the Jupiter II in *Lost in Space.*

While Burke makes like MacGyver and builds a battery from scratch, Virdon finds himself in a manufactured domestic situation that reminds him of his own family, just as he did in the previous episode, "The Good Seeds." There's a lapse in continuity, however, when Virdon observes, "I'd forgotten what a city looks like," when he had just been in San Francisco in episode #3, "The Trap."

The spotlight in these early episodes remains on the two astronauts, which is odd considering how Roddy McDowall is top-billed in the series and the show's most substantial link with the *Apes* movies. Galen's role is almost incidental here, though he has a nice moment while staring with wonderment at the ancient computers: "How," he wonders, "could man ever have known so much and done so little with it?"

Though Urko has the guns and the soldiers, Dr. Zaius again proves the more dangerous adversary here because of his insight into human psychology. With Zaius the war is not against humans, but against the spread of their philosophy that humans are the equal of apes and were once their superiors in a bygone day. In "The Legacy," Booth Colman comes into his own, proving himself the equal of Maurice Evans in what is perhaps the most pivotal role in the mythos.

Ron Harper, who recalled "The Legacy" as one of his favorite episodes, revealed that the photograph Virdon carried of his wife was originally a picture of Harper's wife, actress Sally Stark. But when blonde beauty Zina Bethune was cast as Arn, producers replaced the photo of Stark, a brunette, with another blonde, to reinforce the connection between the two women in the story.

EPISODE SIX: TOMORROW'S TIDE
Original Airdate: October 18, 1974
Produced by: Stan Hough
Written by: Robert W. Lenski
Directed by: Don McDougall

Guest Stars: Roscoe Lee Browne (Hurton), Jay Robinson (Bandor), Kathleen Bracken (Soma), Jim Storm (Romar), John McLaim (Gahto).

Burke and Virdon rescue an old man who had been tied to a raft and set adrift. By the metal bracelet he wears, Galen identifies him as an inmate from a labor camp. The two astronauts are captured by the camp's tough commandant and, after a frightening trial by fire, are forced to work as fishermen.

Commentary
The first real clunker in the run, "Tomorrow's Tide" plays like one

For Ron Harper, *Planet of the Apes* was the fifth attempt at a successful TV series (Globe Photos).

long excuse for Ron Harper and James Naughton to take off their shirts. Perhaps the beefcake ploy worked with female viewers, but there's not much else going on in the story. Give credit to the stars, however, for performing many of their own stunts in the underwater scenes. The only amusing moments emerge from the testing of Galen's patience, when he is left in charge of the man rescued by Burke and Virdon.

Jay Robinson, yet another connection to the Ruby/Spears era of Krofft television, plays Bandor, the Ape second-in-command. Though his face is buried beneath the usual simian appliances, the sinister melodic voice that once belonged to "Dr. Shrinker" is immediately recognizable.

EPISODE SEVEN: THE SURGEON

Original Airdate: October 25, 1974
Produced by: Stan Hough
Written by: Barry Oringer
Directed by: Arnold Laven

Guest Stars: Jacqueline Scott (Kira), Michael Strong (Travin), Martin Brooks (Leander), Jamie Smith Jackson (Girl), David Naughton (Dr. Stole), Raymond Mayo (Human), Diana Hale (Brigid), Phil Montgomery (Jordo).

Virdon is shot by a gorilla patrol. Galen contacts Kira, his ex-fiancée and chief surgeon at the planet's best medical facility. She agrees to help, but cannot save Alan's life without a book on human anatomy, and the only one known to exist is in the office of Dr. Zaius. A daring deception secures the book. Kira realizes that Virdon will need a blood transfusion to survive, and must overcome the prejudices of her ape colleagues to perform the procedure.

Commentary

With the exception of the pilot episode "Escape From Tomorrow," "The Surgeon" is as good as it got in the television chapter of the *Planet of the Apes* saga. Much of the credit belongs to guest star Jacqueline Scott, who makes her second series appearance (see "The Good Seeds"). She plays Kira, a brilliant doctor whose life is relatively uncomplicated until Galen's return.

After a humorous early scene, in which we learn something about ape pick-up lines (offers of vegetable casserole do wonders, apparently), Kira is confronted with a situation that causes her to question everything she's ever learned about apes and humans. Like Dr. Zira in the first *Apes* movie, she discovers the truth about human prehistory, and Zaius's role in suppressing the information. When she attempts to explain a blood transfusion to apes and humans, two species ruled by superstition, Barry Oringer's script touches upon themes of science vs. folklore, and history vs. religion, the same conflicts faced by scientists from Copernicus to Darwin. Pretty heady stuff for a weekly adventure series, but perfectly consistent with the lofty aspirations of the films.

David Naughton, brother of James Naughton and the star of *An American Werewolf in London* (1981), appears as Kira's colleague, Dr. Stole.

EPISODE EIGHT: THE DECEPTION
Original Airdate: November 1, 1974
Produced by: Stan Hough
Written by: Anthony Lawrence, Ken Spears, and Joe Ruby; Story by Anthony Lawrence
Directed by: Don McDougall

Guest Stars: Jane Actman (Fauna), Pat Renella (Zon), John Milford (Sestus), Hal Baylor (Jasko), Baynes Barron (Perdix).

After a beloved ape, Lucian, is killed by a human, a group of vigilante apes known as the Dragoons raid human villages, burning homes and killing anyone who dares fight back. Burke and Virdon attempt to find the killer, in the hopes of ending the raids. They are given shelter by Fauna, the blind daughter of Lucian. Galen introduces his two friends as apes, because Fauna now fears and hates all human beings. While Galen infiltrates the Dragoons, Fauna falls in love with Burke.

Commentary
"It almost makes me ashamed to be an ape," says Galen after viewing the destruction caused by the hooded Dragoons, who are clearly meant to represent hate groups like the Ku Klux Klan. Prejudice and intolerance are familiar themes in the world of *Planet of the Apes*, but here they're played out with a rather tired cliché, the blind girl who cannot see skin color (or in this case, fur covering) and realizes her hatred towards humans is groundless.

It's also no surprise that the actual killer of Lucian turns out to be an ape.

In this, as in other unspectacular episodes, it's the performance of Roddy McDowall as Galen that carries the show. His rescue of Burke and Virdon after they are apprehended by the ape police is one of the funniest scenes in the series; later, when he learns that Fauna has fallen for Burke, his anger at Burke's actions is unexpectedly intense.

EPISODE NINE: THE HORSE RACE

Original Airdate: November 8, 1974
Produced by: Stan Hough
Written by: David P. Lewis and Booker Bradshaw
Directed by: Jack Starrett

Guest Stars: Morgan Woodward (Martin), John Hoyt (Barlow), Richard Devon (Zandar), Henry Levin (Prefect), Russ Marin (Damon), Meegan King (Gregor).

Urko wagers the prefects of different villages that his champion horse and rider can defeat their best in a race, and wins every time through treachery. After the race in a village where Burke and Virdon are hiding, Galen is bitten by a lethal scorpion. Gregor, son of the local blacksmith, rides to the village to retrieve an antidote. His mission is successful, but Gregor is sentenced to execution for violating the law against humans riding horses. Galen appeals to the prefect, who offers a bargain: he will spare Gregor's life if a rider can be found to defeat General Urko's champion. Virdon agrees to take the challenge, and must not only win the race, but avoid being captured by the General's troops.

Commentary

The "big race" is another staple of adventure series, whether it's staged on foot, in cars, on horses, or in spaceships. "The Horse Race" doesn't add much to the familiar formula.

As the season progressed, the apes were toned down somewhat as adversaries, a response to network concern over the level of violence in the series. The General Urko in this episode is not the same bloodthirsty soldier he was in "The Trap." He's also not the same honorable, albeit intolerant adversary. A once proud warrior, he has been reduced here to petty tyrant, swindling his own species out of their horses and lands.

There are two running gags in the *Planet of the Apes* series, and they're both in this episode: Galen's delight in masquerading as the owner of Burke and Virdon, and his amusing confusion at the astronauts' 20th-century colloquialisms.

John Hoyt returns as Prefect Barlow, who was introduced in "The Gladiators" (#2).

EPISODE TEN: THE INTERROGATION
Original Airdate: November 15, 1974
Produced by: Stan Hough
Written by: Richard Collins
Directed by: Alf Kjellin

Guest Stars: Beverly Garland (Wanda), Anne Seymour (Ann), Norman Burton (Yalu), Lee Delano (Officer Gorilla), Wayne Foster (Lt. Gorilla), Lynn Benesch (Susan), Harry Townes (Dr. Malthus).

Burke is captured by Urko's soldiers, and subjected to an experimental form of brainwashing by Wanda, a prominent doctor. While Galen and Virdon form a rescue plan, Burke is repeatedly asked to divulge the names of every human that has offered him assistance. After successfully resisting the treatment, he is turned over to Urko for execution.

Commentary
The main storyline of Richard Collins' script is not nearly as interesting as the subplot, in which Galen is reunited with his parents. Anne Seymour stars as the chimp's kindly mother, Ann, and

Norman Burton, a veteran of the *Apes* movie series, portrays his gruff father, Counselor Yalu. Another nice scene has the delusional Burke remembering in flashback his life on earth prior to being launched into the future; James Naughton finally gets to wear something other than his standard blue tunic and brown khakis.

The interrogation in the title is a bust, though Urko's interpretation of "brainwashing" is amusing: "That's when you take the brain out of the skull and wash it with cool water." Sadistic doctor Wanda is played by Beverly Garland, known as the "Queen of the 'B's'" for her appearances in movies such as *The Neanderthal Man* (1953), *Curucu, Beast of the Amazon* (1956), and *The Alligator People* (1959). With all the bizarre creatures she's encountered in her four-decade career, Garland is one of the few actresses for whom playing the role of a talking ape would not be considered a departure.

EPISODE ELEVEN: THE TYRANT
Original Airdate: November 22, 1974
Produced by: Stan Hough
Written by: Walter Black
Directed by: Ralph Senensky

Guest Stars: Percy Rodrigues (Aboro), Michael Conrad (Janor), Joseph Ruskin (Daku), Klair Bybee (Sam), Arlen Stuart (Gola), James Naughton (Mikal).

Burke and Virdon come to the aid of impoverished farmers, who are being taxed at an exorbitant rate by the local district chief, Aboro. When the despotic chief tries to expand the territory under his control, the astronauts and Galen use deception to manufacture a power struggle between Aboro and Urko, in the hope of removing the tyrant from power.

Commentary

One of the more violent episodes in the run, "The Tyrant" features Percy Rodrigues in a ferocious performance as Aboro, whose methods are so abhorrent that they actually prompt a mid-episode truce between the astronauts and General Urko. The moment recalls scenes in *The Fugitive* when Lt. Gerard was forced to work with Richard Kimble, and any such moments that shake up the old formula are always welcome. However, Aboro's line "Urko never really approved of corruption," conflicts with the gorilla General's actions in "The Horse Race."

Roddy McDowall has a stand-out scene when Galen goes undercover as Zaius's assistant, Octavius, with help from his cousin, Augustus. But the plot device of Galen just happening to know a prefect/doctor/relative in every new village is becoming overused.

Michael Conrad, an Emmy winner for *Hill Street Blues* in 1981, plays Janor, one of the persecuted villagers.

EPISODE TWELVE: THE CURE

Original Airdate: November 29, 1974
Produced by: Stan Hough
Written by: Edward J. Lakso
Directed by: Bernard McEveety

Guest Stars: Sondra Locke (Amy), David Sheiner (Zoran), Ron Soble (Kava), George Wallace (Talbert), Biff Elliot (Orangutan), Albert Cole (Mason), Ron Stein (Neesa), Charles Leland (Dying Man).

Virdon is sad to leave Amy, a lovely young woman, but realizes he and his companions cannot remain in one village for long if they hope to avoid General Urko. But shortly after the fugitives' departure, Amy's village is quarantined, and several residents quickly succumb to an unknown illness. Virdon is concerned that the virus may have started with him and Burke, but after returning they realize it's malaria.

After Amy falls ill, the astronauts try to locate a natural source of quinine, which will cure the disease. But Urko, who has surrounded the village with his troops, urges Dr. Zaius to approve a more permanent solution to the plague — burn everything in sight.

Commentary

Edward Lakso's second script for the series is another winner. Once again, as in "The Trap," Lakso writes General Urko as a warrior whose pride will not be undermined. He nearly attempts to overthrow Dr. Zaius here, in his zeal to not be proven wrong about the malady in the quarantined village.

Blonde beauty Sondra Locke plays Amy, the girl who falls for Virdon and unwittingly reveals his true history to an ape doctor. Locke's performance here just barely predates her first meeting with Clint Eastwood, with whom she would appear in a succession of action features, including *The Gauntlet* (1977) and *Sudden Impact* (1983).

EPISODE THIRTEEN: THE LIBERATOR

Original Airdate: None
Produced by: Stan Hough
Written by: Howard Dimsdale
Directed by: Arnold Laven

Guest Stars: John Ireland (Brun), Ben Andrews (Miro), Jennifer Ashley (Talia), Peter G. Skinner (Clim), Mark Bailey (Villager), Ron Stein (1st Gorilla Guard), Tom McDonough (2nd Gorilla Guard).

Burke and Virdon are captured by the inhabitants of a village that is forced to surrender ten people every month to a squad of apes, so they can be put to work in the mines. When Galen's influence cannot secure their release, the astronauts must convince their captors that their best hope for the future is to rebel against the apes who enslave them.

Commentary

"The Liberator" is a reworking of *The Lottery*, a famous Shirley Jackson short story that almost everybody reads in high school. The episode was never aired in the U.S. It debuted in England the following year, and was subsequently restored to the rerun package when the series aired on the Sci-Fi Channel. But in 1974, when VCRs were a $1,000 luxury and there weren't 50 cable stations airing old network castoffs, *Planet of the Apes* fans could only wonder about what they were missing.

Those who waited decades to see "The Liberator" probably thought it was worth the wait. Burke and Virdon face a formidable challenge in changing the deeply ingrained traditions of subservience among the villagers. These astronauts aren't restricted by a prime directive like the *Star Trek* crew; their mission is to open the minds of the villagers and break centuries-old traditions, supposedly ordained by ancient gods. Along the way there are several Thanksgiving references, which suggest when the episode was originally supposed to air. At one point the jailed astronauts worry about being "stuffed like a Thanksgiving turkey," and later hope the pretty girl who serves their meals will "be our Pocahontas."

John Ireland's performance as Brun is one of the most memorable guest appearances on the series. At first he appears to be a man of quiet integrity trapped in a no-win situation, but gradually his façade is stripped away to reveal a lunatic plotting genocide.

EPISODE FOURTEEN:
UP ABOVE THE WORLD SO HIGH

Original Airdate: December 20, 1974
Produced by: Stan Hough
Written by: S. Bar-David and Arthur Browne, Jr.
Story by: S. Bar-David
Directed by: John Meredyth Lucas

Guest Stars: Joanna Barnes (Carsia), Frank Aletter (Leuric),

Martin Brooks (Konag), William Beckley (Council Orang), Ron Stein (Gorilla Guard), Eldon Burke (2nd Trooper), Glenn Wilder (Human Driver).

The fugitive trio are astonished to see a man flying with a home-made glider. They rush to the site where the glider crashes, and find the man, Leuric, obsessed with making another attempt to soar through the skies. But before he can try he is captured by the apes and taken to Central City. Urko and Dr. Zaius want Leuric killed, but Carsia, a chimpanzee scientist, suggests that he build another glider, which could be used by the apes. Burke and Virdon help Leuric in secret, unaware that Carsia has a more sinister hidden objective in saving Leuric's life.

Commentary

There was much to admire in the *Planet of the Apes* TV series, but apparently not enough to attract viewers away from *Sanford and Son* or *Chico and the Man*. The programmers at CBS swing an even bigger axe than General Urko, and let it fall on the series after just one season. We'll never know where they would take the characters next, but the final episode, "Up Above the World So High," offers evidence of which story elements might have sustained the show for another season, and which would have to be phased out or significantly changed.

The culture-clash between man and ape, played straight in the film series with calamitous consequences, received a lighter treatment in the relationship between Burke and Virdon and their chimpanzee friend, Galen. This episode's best scene has the astronauts talking Galen into taking the first test flight in their new glider. Long accustomed to intellectual superiority over the planet's humans, Galen now realizes how much he can learn from his companions, and how he must trust them if they are all to survive. The dynamic of their friendship had many unexplored possibilities, that could have sustained many more stories.

The use of hang-gliders in the story was intriguing, and

suggests countless story ideas. The astronauts could have introduced 20th-century technology to the human villagers in an attempt to advance their society and place them on a more equal footing with their ape rulers.

However, the characters of the apes in charge were beginning to border on the ridiculous, and required a change. "How could a human idea serve us?" asks an incredulous General Urko when Carsia urges the council to let Leuric build another flying machine. Urko's complete dismissal of the human race is a device used over and over, and grew less convincing with every new example of the astronauts' ingenuity. After being repeatedly outsmarted by Burke and Virdon, the apes may have continued their public denials of the humans' intelligence to maintain the status quo, but privately they should have known better. By this episode, Urko and even Dr. Zaius sound like Agent Scully in early seasons of the *The X-Files*, still denying the supernatural after witnessing dozens of paranormal incidents.

RETURN TO THE PLANET OF THE APES

Animated series

NBC

Saturday, September 6, 1975–Saturday, September 4, 1976, 11–11:30 a.m.

Produced by David H. DePatie and Friz Freleng, based on characters created by Pierre Boulle; Directed by Doug Wildey; Music by Dean Elliott and Eric Rogers

CAST:

Richard Blackburn (Zaius/Bill Hudson)
Henry Corden (General Urko)
Edwin Mills (Cornelius)
Claudette Nevins (Judy Franklin/Nova)

Phillippa Harris (Zira)
Austin Stoker (Jeff Carter)

Return to the Planet of the Apes is the least-celebrated chapter in the ongoing saga based on *Monkey Planet,* but ironically it's also the only adaptation that depicts simian society as it was originally envisioned by Pierre Boulle. Budget restrictions prevented the *Planet of the Apes* films from portraying the apes as technologically advanced. But in cartoons it costs the same to draw high-tech cities as it does primitive settlements, so for the first time the apes were given all the modern comforts ascribed to them by their creator, including automobiles, movie theaters, and television sets.

Although set in the distant future, Ape City in this animated series is an odd amalgam of different historical eras. The building's architecture resembles ancient Rome, the cars have body designs from the 1940s and 1950s, and the military uses state-of-the-art weaponry. Likewise, the cast of characters are a mishmash of those from Boulle's novel, a few from the films and live-action television series, and a new band of human explorers who find themselves in the same predicament as Charlton Heston and James Franciscus.

Dr. Zaius, Cornelius, and Zira are back, and will be recognizable to fans who only know them from the features. Once again, it is Zaius who knows the true history of the planet, and conceals its heritage for the good of his species. The two chimpanzee scientists are, as always, sympathetic to the human cause and tireless advocates for peace between the races. They are opposed by General Urko, who first appeared in the CBS-TV series, and believes the only good human is a dead human. Nova makes an appearance, as does an astronaut named Brent, and a race of subterranean humans with telepathic powers. The most prominent new characters are astronauts Bill Hudson, Jeff Carter, and Judy Franklin, who crash on the planet in the grand tradition of their NASA predecessors.

None of the characters from previous *Apes* projects were voiced by the actors who originally portrayed them. The cast was comprised mostly of newcomers to voice animation, with the exception of Henry Corden, whose distinguished résumé includes such cartoon icons as Fred Flintstone, and voice work in the Saturday morning classics *The Banana Splits Adventure Hour* and *Josie and the Pussycats*. It's interesting to note that Austin Stoker, who provided the voice for Jeff Carter, also played MacDonald in the final film, *Battle for the Planet of the Apes*.

"We taped the episodes together — to do a good acting job, you had to have everybody there so we could react vocally to each other," recalls Henry Corden. "Usually there was a quick rehearsal — maybe an hour — and we'd change a few lines, then it was into the studio, where we'd take another hour and a half to tape an episode."

By 1970s' animation standards, *Return to the Planet of the Apes* falls short of other series airing at that time, such as *Devlin* or *The Super Friends*. Establishing shots feature wonderfully detailed painted images of Ape City, but there's very little movement by the characters in the frame. Such deficiencies are surprising from a show that lists Friz Freleng and Doug Wildey among its creative talent. Wildey was instrumental in creating the cartoon adventure series *Johnny Quest;* Freleng's name is familiar to any animation aficionado, as the creator of Porky Pig and the Pink Panther, and one of the geniuses at Warner Bros. during the halcyon days of *Looney Tunes* and *Merrie Melodies*.

The most curious name in the credits, however, belongs to MacDonald Stearns, Ph.D., UCLA Department of Germanic Languages, who was hired to research "anthropological dialogue." I have no idea what he actually contributed, since all the characters use simple 20th-century parlance, and none of the humans or apes speak German.

The story is told in serial format. Situations and ideas are introduced and left unresolved for several episodes, which demands a viewer loyalty not common to the average sugar-coated-cereal-crunching viewer of '70s-era Saturday morning TV. *Return to the Planet of the Apes* also deals with several sophisticated concepts, including the usual *Planet of the Apes* standbys of racial harmony, religious tolerance, and pacifism. The combination of highbrow stories and primitive animation results in a series that fails to appeal to either older or younger viewers.

Return to the Planet of the Apes debuted at 11 a.m. and went up against two live-action shows: The Sid & Marty Krofft entry *Far Out Space Nuts* on CBS, and *Uncle Croc's Block*, starring Charles Nelson Reilly, on ABC. The latter was canceled in February of 1976, and replaced by reruns of the cartoon *Sabrina and the Groovy Ghoulies*. The apes could not outdraw even this questionable competition, and was canceled after one season. Since then, the series has been rediscovered by *Planet of the Apes* fans, and has aired occasionally on the Sci-Fi Channel.

EPISODE GUIDE

EPISODE ONE: FLAMES OF DOOM
Written by: Larry Spiegel

On the NASA spacecraft Venturer, astronaut Bill Hudson and his crew, Jeff Carter and Judy Franklin, attempt to test a theory of "time-thrust" advanced by the distinguished Dr. Stanton. Having left earth in 1979, they realize after traveling 100 years into the future that their experiment has been a success. Suddenly, however, they lose control of the craft, which crashes on a desolate planet. According to the Venturer's clock, the year is now 3979.

After enduring electrical storms, earthquakes, and mysterious walls of fire that incinerate their survival packs, the astronauts are separated when Judy falls through a fissure in the planet's surface. Bill and Jeff head for higher ground to search for her, and spot a band of primitive humans in the distance. They are unable to communicate with them, but after collapsing from exhaustion the humans carry the two astronauts back to their settlement.

When they revive, they notice one of the women, Nova, wearing the I.D. tags of an astronaut named Brent, who was born more than a century after the Venturer began its journey. Before they can learn any more, the settlement is attacked by uniformed apes on horseback. Nova hides with Jeff, but Bill is captured and taken to Ape City.

Bill stares in wonder at the modern, technically advanced city run by intelligent apes, unaware that General Urko, leader of the gorilla army, has petitioned the city's Supreme Council for permission to exterminate all humans. He is opposed by the chimpanzee Cornelius, an animal psychologist who argues for allowing the humans to survive as subjects of scientific research. The Council rules that humans need not be annihilated unless they learn the power of speech, which, according to the Book of Simian Prophecy, would lead to the destruction of the planet.

Commentary

The natural disasters on the planet are the same as those encountered by Taylor and Nova in *Beneath the Planet of the Apes*. These calamities and the disappearance of Judy, which parallels the disappearance of Taylor in *Beneath*, neatly foreshadow the first appearance of the mutants in a later episode.

There's another connection with *Beneath* in the introduction of a relationship between Nova and an astronaut named Brent, though the two characters are similar in name only.

EPISODE TWO: ESCAPE FROM APE CITY
Written by: Larry Spiegel

Bill is warned not to speak by other humans captured in the gorilla raid. He is turned over to scientists Cornelius and Zira for study, despite General Urko's objections. Jeff and Nova, having hidden from the gorillas' attack, follow the captured humans to Ape City, hoping to rescue their friend.

Zira subjects Bill to a series of tests, and is delighted by his abilities; she nicknames him "Blue Eyes." Dr. Zaius, head of the Supreme Council, is less than enthusiastic about the human's intelligence. When Cornelius suggests subjecting Bill to a brain probe, the astronaut can no longer remain silent. Zira and Cornelius are shocked by his ability to talk. Bill's explanation of who he is and where he came from is overheard by one of Urko's soldiers, who reports his discovery to the Council. A frightened Dr. Zaius orders all humans destroyed. When they hear the news, Zira and Cornelius help Bill to escape. He meets Jeff and Nova on the outskirts of the city, and together they steal a truck and race toward the Forbidden Zone, hoping to retrieve a laser from their spaceship.

Commentary

"Escape from Ape City" reintroduces several characters from previous *Apes* projects. Their voices are all provided by different actors, many of whom seem to be attempting an imitation of their film/television counterparts. Phillippa Harris's performance as Zira in particular sounds remarkably like that of Kim Hunter. Her reference to Bill as "Blue Eyes" recalls Hunter's Zira naming Taylor "Bright Eyes" in *Planet of the Apes*.

One of the animated series' most confusing quirks is the reference to humans as "humanoids." Even Bill and Jeff refer to their fellow citizens as humanoid, which means a creature who appears to be, but is not, human. The designation might be understandable when the astronauts are unaware that they're back on earth, but even after their location is revealed (in episode five), the astronauts don't abandon the habit.

EPISODE THREE: LAGOON OF PERIL

Written by: J. C. Strong

Evidence mounts against the intelligent humans. One of General Urko's soldiers reports having seen a spacecraft crash in the desert, and three oddly-garbed humans emerge from within. However, the Lawgiver overrules Urko and Dr. Zaius, and rescinds the order calling for human genocide. Zaius and Urko lead an expedition into the Forbidden Zone to retrieve evidence of the soldier's allegation, but are hampered in their journey by fire and lightning.

Cornelius and Zira send a message to Bill and Jeff, to warn them of their danger. They explain that if the ship is found, Urko's theory that Bill and Jeff have "infected" other humans with the ability to think will be supported by the government, and the extermination of humans will begin. The astronauts reach their ship before the ape expedition and retrieve the laser, after battling a giant sea serpent. They destroy the ship.

When the army arrives they see the serpent, and Zaius concludes that the soldier confused the creature for a spacecraft, and that the rumors of intelligent humans are false.

Commentary

For many viewers, the most entertaining aspect of the animated series is the silly little moments that are often incidental to the main plot. In "Lagoon of Peril," for instance, there's an amusing special report from the Ape Broadcasting System, delivered by a mustachioed ape named Dick Huntley (a send-up of long-time NBC anchorman Chet Huntley).

The scene in which Dr. Zaius explains the Forbidden Zone illusions is straight out of *Beneath the Planet of the Apes*. As the voice of Zaius, Richard Blackburn effectively emulates the melodious Shakespearian tones of Maurice Evans. The most annoying voice in the series belongs to Nova (Claudette Nevins), who fortunately doesn't speak very often. But here, her constant cries of "A-ho-ya!" sound like a shrill fusion of Judy Tenuta and Pebbles Flintstone.

The voice of Claudette Nevins graced the animated *Planet of the Apes* series, as both Judy Franklin and Nova (Globe Photos).

EPISODE FOUR: TUNNEL OF FEAR

Written by: Larry Spiegel

The astronauts hatch a plan to move the humans to a new settlement that will be safe from Urko's patrols. They sneak into Ape City to meet with Cornelius and Zira, hoping they will help them. The two scientists, already under suspicion by Dr. Zaius of being sympathetic to the human cause, hesitate to commit any further act that might be considered treason by the Supreme Council. However, Cornelius tells Bill and Jeff about a valley near one of his archaeological digs that might be suitable.

The next day, it is decided that a river route to the valley would be the best way to avoid gorilla pursuit. The astronauts drift past the ruins of an ancient civilization, and after a harrowing plunge down a waterfall they reach the human settlement.

Commentary

Near the beginning of "Tunnel of Fear," there's a sequence featuring an ape farmer garbed in overalls, listening to ape country music, carrying a load of hay in a red pick-up truck, that is irresistibly funny. Less obvious but no less amusing is Bill and Jeff's remarkable good fortune when they travel to Ape City, a metropolis the size of New York judging from the aerial view that appears in this episode, in search of Cornelius and Zira. They reach the city via sewer pipe, and out of thousands of manhole (apehole?) covers they manage to pop through the one right outside Zira's lab. What luck!

In scenes featuring Cornelius guiding the astronauts back to their settlement, there are several references to "Hidden Valley," which sounds like a salad dressing. In subsequent shows, the humans' new home is wisely changed to "New Valley."

EPISODE FIVE: THE UNEARTHLY PROPHECY

Written by: Jack Kaplan and John Barrett

Bill and Jeff are spotted in the desert by General Urko and his army. The astronauts escape through an underground passage that materializes out of nowhere, then disappears after Bill and Jeff are safely inside. Urko suspects the Underdwellers, a mysterious race of subterranean beings, of helping the astronauts.

In an underground cavern, Bill and Jeff find the ruins of the New York Public Library, Wall Street, and Times Square. They realize that they've been on earth all along. Later, they are met by cloaked, hooded figures chanting, "USA." Following the figures into a large cavern, Bill and Jeff see their missing comrade, Judy, also garbed in the Underdwellers' robes. She ignores their cries, and does not react when the astronauts are stunned by a ray gun and locked in prison.

Krador, ruler of the Underdwellers, tells Bill and Jeff that the arrival of Judy fulfills a prophecy among his people of a leader named "USA" that will help them return to the surface world. The "USA" emblazoned on Judy's astronaut uniform was proof that she would be their guide. Later, Jeff gives Judy a ring which revives her memory. She helps her friends escape, but is unable to resist Krador's telepathic power, and returns to the underground cavern. Bill and Jeff vow to rescue their friend as soon as they can.

Commentary

"The Unearthly Prophecy" contains two major revelations in the story arc of the series: the astronauts' realization that they're back on earth, and their reunion with Judy. Both dramatic developments offer the opportunity for heightened performances among the cast, but Bill and Jeff recover rather quickly from the back-to-back shocks, and the scenes aren't played for all they're worth.

The animated series mined many of its most significant story nuggets from *Beneath the Planet of the Apes*, as evidenced here by the introduction of the Underdwellers, whose hooded cloaks and telepathic powers are reminiscent of the mutants encountered by Brent and Nova. For fans of the films who just want to sample the animated series, this fast-paced, well-written episode is your best bet.

EPISODE SIX: TERROR ON ICE MOUNTAIN
Written by: Bruce Shelly
Cornelius unearths an ancient book called "A Day at the Zoo," which depicts apes behind bars for the amusement of a human civilization. Recognizing the danger of possessing such a book, and the truth it contains, Cornelius realizes it can never fall into the hands of Urko or Zaius. Unable to find a safe hiding place, he then discovers that the paper used to wrap the book is actually a blueprint for a hot-air balloon. With help from Bill and Jeff, he builds the balloon and casts off with Bill for the snow-covered mountain of Ghar, where he is certain the book will be safe.

The balloon crashes en route, and its descent is spotted by Urko's troopers. Cornelius and Bill are sheltered by the temple of Kigor, god of the mountain apes. While the balloon is repaired, Kigor defends the temple's inhabitants against the gorillas. The temple's High Llama agrees to keep the book in a secret cave.

Commentary

It's a stretch to build an entire episode around Cornelius's attempt to hide a book, but "Terror on Ice Mountain" does contain a couple of interesting visuals. The wintry mountain backdrop is a new one for any *Apes* project, as are gorilla troops on skis. The Zen philosophies espoused by the High Llama in his Tibetan style temple are pretty sophisticated stuff for a Saturday morning cartoon.

EPISODE SEVEN: RIVER OF FLAMES

Written by: Jack Kaplan and John Barrett

Judy urges Bill and Jeff to return with her to the Underdwellers' home, where a lava flow threatens to destroy the entire settlement if it reaches the reactor room. While the astronauts try to save the Underdwellers, Urko debates with Zira and Cornelius over the allocation of public funds, and whether they should be spent on national defense or scientific research.

The astronauts retrieve their laser, after it is stolen by Urko's troops. They use it to create an alternate path in the mountain-side so the lava can be released safely. In gratitude for their efforts, Krador allows Judy to depart with them, as long as she agrees to return when USA is needed.

Dr. Zaius sides with the scientists, leaving Urko only enough money to replace all the military equipment he has lost while tracking the astronauts.

Commentary

Judy has now emerged as the series' most interesting character. Still loyal to Bill and Jeff, she has also accepted the responsibility thrust upon her by Krador as USA of the Underdwellers. Otherwise, "River of Flames" is a standard episode, with the occasional clever pop culture reference (two apes talk about seeing that new hit movie, "The Ape-Father"), and Urko still chasing but never catching Bill and Jeff. Despite Henry Corden's best effort, however, it's hard for the General to sound tough and mean when he declares his intention to "hunt down Blue Eyes."

EPISODE EIGHT: SCREAMING WINGS
Written by: Jack Kaplan and John Barrett

Bill, Jeff, and Judy, together again, are surprised to see a World War II P-40 fighter plane, piloted by an ape, engaged in target practice on human dummies. Bill fears that aerial capability will make Urko's army invincible, and plots to steal the plane with the help of Cornelius. Cornelius, who believes Urko might one day use the plane to attack apes as well, agrees to help the astronauts in their mission.

While Bill and Jeff incapacitate the pilot, Judy jumps into the cockpit and flies away with the aircraft. She drops a net on General Urko and his men to prevent them from capturing her friends, who send a locomotive crashing into the apes' aircraft factory, leaving them unable to build any more planes. An outraged Dr. Zaius proposes an investigation into Urko's fitness to command, and reasserts his suspicions of Cornelius and Zira helping the human fugitives.

Commentary
"Screaming Wings" is the first episode since the pilot to feature Bill, Jeff, and Judy working together as a team. Judy finally meets Cornelius and Zira, in a scene that should have had more impact. Another missed opportunity comes when Judy, at the controls of the P-40, drops a net on General Urko, a moment that could easily have been turned into something fun with a few witty lines of dialogue. But writers Jack Kaplan and John Barrett ignore the chance to inject some much-needed humor into an otherwise somber story.

EPISODE NINE: TRAIL TO THE UNKNOWN

Written by: Larry Spiegel

Preparations to move the human settlement to New Valley are completed, and the tribe, led by Bill, Jeff, and Judy, journey by raft to their new home. They pass through deserts and jungles fraught with peril, until they reach the end of the river and must set out on foot. On the way, they find the remains of a US spaceship, and meet its pilot, Ron Brent.

Brent explains that he landed on the planet after leaving earth in the year 2019. He was met by Nova's tribe, but was later separated from them by a natural disaster. He has been in the same spot, alone, for more than 20 years, and eagerly agrees to join the expedition that soon reaches New Valley. Using their ship's laser, Bill and Jeff build a fortress that is completed just as General Urko's army attacks. The fortress holds, and Urko must return to Ape City for heavier artillery. Realizing the army will soon be back, Bill decides to destroy the land bridge into the valley.

Commentary

The first appearance of Brent, whose character was mentioned as far back as Episode One, is the highlight of this stand-out episode. The most amusing moment occurs when Judy says, "Nova tells me some of the humanoids have become ill," which is odd because Nova hasn't said a word to anyone else all this time except for "A-ho-ya!" Maybe Judy's time with the Underdwellers has made her bilingual.

EPISODE TEN: ATTACK FROM THE CLOUDS

Written by: Larry Spiegel

The astronauts retrieve the P-40 fighter plane from a secret location, hoping to use it to destroy the land bridge to New Valley. However, they must first deal with another menace from the skies: a giant monster bird that attacks the human settlement. While Jeff leads the humans to safe haven inside a cave, Bill and Judy engage in a furious dogfight with the creature. After striking the monster with the plane's landing gear, the beast plummets into a lake, but miraculously survives the fall.

Commentary

The "monster bird" is a ridiculous-looking creature, with an even more ridiculous name. The most intriguing aspect in the story is Dr. Zaius's informal alliance with Cornelius and Zira, against the machinations of General Urko.

EPISODE ELEVEN: MISSION OF MERCY

Written by: Larry Spiegel

The dogfight with the monster has left the airplane low on fuel, so Bill and Jeff risk another journey into Ape City to replenish their supply. While they are gone, Nova falls deathly ill from a disease Brent identifies as Acute Infectious Streptococholus. Without treatment, Nova will perish in 72 hours. Judy flies to Ape City, where Cornelius and Zira mix a serum that will cure the disease. However, she does not have enough fuel to return to New Valley. With the help of their chimpanzee friends, the astronauts rendezvous at a secluded farmhouse. Bill and Jeff arrive by truck carrying a fresh fuel supply, and they all return to New Valley in time to save Nova.

Commentary

With this episode, *Return to the Planet of the Apes* secures a place for itself in the history of Saturday morning cartoons, as the only series to use Acute Infectious Streptococholus as a plot device. Despite the medical double-talk there's a lot of action in this one, as the astronauts are chased by Urko's army on land and in the air, as they race against time to bring life-saving medicine to New Valley.

EPISODE TWELVE:
INVASION OF THE UNDERDWELLERS

Written by: J. C. Strong

Homes, museums, and libraries in Ape City are being robbed of their most precious possessions, and suspicion falls on the Underdwellers. In reality, the thieves are General Urko and his gorilla soldiers, who plan to frame the Underdwellers to justify an invasion of their world. Krador appears to Bill, Jeff, and Judy, and tells them his people are innocent.

Dr. Zaius declares war on the Underdwellers. Urko assures the Council that he can end the war quickly by blowing up the tunnels that lead to the underground caverns. The astronauts find the stolen merchandise, and uncover Urko's scheme. Using Krador's telepathic powers, Bill's image is beamed to Cornelius and Zira. He tells the two chimpanzees to take Zaius to the tomb where Urko stashed the stolen property. Once he realizes what has happened, Zaius relieves Urko of command.

Commentary

Urko finally crosses the line in his obsession with military rule. He not only violates a sacred law against stealing from a fellow ape, he nearly destroys Ape City by threatening to detonate the tunnels that run beneath the city. "Invasion of the Underdwellers" contains Urko's comeuppance from Dr. Zaius, the return of the Underdwellers, and Judy assuming her "USA" persona. All that, plus a reference to the great writer "William Apespeare."

EPISODE THIRTEEN: BATTLE OF THE TITANS

Written by: Bruce Shelly

Cornelius and Zira are convinced that the time is right to retrieve the book they had hidden with the High Llama, revealing man's history on earth, and show it to the Supreme Council. Only then, they believe, will laws be passed to protect mankind. Cornelius and Bill consult on how best to return to Kigor's mountain. They decide to rebuild the hot air balloon that carried them there the first time. But on their way to the mountain, their balloon is attacked by the monster bird.

General Urko, relieved of his command, tells the army to obey his successor, Colonel Rotok. But he refuses to wait any longer to launch another invasion on the humans' fortress. When the gorillas attack, Judy manages to get to the airplane, and drive Rotok's forces back with an aerial assault.

Bill and Cornelius survive the monster bird attack and reach the High Llama's temple. They recover the book and, after Kigor ends the menace of the monster bird once and for all, they journey home, hoping to finally bring peace and unity to the planet.

Commentary

"Battle of the Titans," the final episode of *Return to the Planet of the Apes*, ties up several dangling story threads, such as the ancient book and the fate of the monster bird, and ends with the astronauts and the chimpanzees on the verge of changing the history of the planet. Sadly, however, we'll never know where the writers would have taken the story from there.

BEHIND THE PLANET OF THE APES

Original Airdate: September 6, 1998
American Movie Classics
120 minutes

Produced by Shelley Lyons, David Comtois and Kevin Burns for Van Ness Films, in association with Foxstar Productions, Twentieth Century Fox Home Entertainment, and American Movie Classics; Written by Brian Anthony, David Comtois, and Kevin Burns; hosted by Roddy McDowall.

Appearances by Mort Abrahams, Frank Capra, Jr., John Chambers, William Creber, Linda Harrison, Charlton Heston,

Kim Hunter, Roddy McDowall, Ricardo Montalban, James Naughton, Ted Post, Don Taylor, J. Lee Thompson, Natalie Trundy, and Richard Zanuck.

The cable television channel American Movie Classics celebrated the 30th anniversary of the release of *Planet of the Apes* with an outstanding documentary, featuring film clips, interviews, and never-before-seen material. Most of the behind-the-scenes footage was shot by host Roddy McDowall, who brought a 16 mm camera with him to the set of *Planet of the Apes* and the three sequels in which he appeared.

Fans can finally see the famous makeup test for the first film, featuring James Brolin, Linda Harrison, and Edward G. Robinson as Dr. Zaius. Also featured is the screen test for the character of a half ape, half human child, originally planned for *Beneath the Planet of the Apes*. On set footage shows the construction of the Statue of Liberty in Malibu, and John Chambers's ape makeup in each stage of application.

Cast and crew interviews contain few surprises, but it's gratifying to hear that the *Planet of the Apes* films are a happy memory for everyone involved in their creation. Most amusing is producer Richard Zanuck's total cluelessness to the films' deeper meanings, which he candidly acknowledges. There's a generous selection of clips from the movies, television series, animated series, and various *Ape* spoofs and tributes.

CHAPTER FOUR

APES IN PRINT

BOOKS

Greene, Eric. *Planet of the Apes as American Myth.*
Jefferson: NC, McFarland, 1996
Eric Greene examines how such issues as race and politics are paramount in the *Planet of the Apes* films and television series. Greene argues that the abuse of Taylor by the apes symbolizes America's fall from grace, and the gorilla army's march into the Forbidden Zone in *Beneath the Planet of the Apes* is a metaphor for U.S. involvement in the Vietnam War. "Greene makes an utterly plausible case for his theory," wrote *Entertainment Weekly* in 1996.

Sausville, Christopher. *Planet of the Apes Collectibles.*
Atglen: PA, Schiffer Publishing Ltd., 1998
A comprehensive price guide to all merchandise, licensed and unlicensed, emerging from the *Planet of the Apes* phenomenon. Dozens of color photos make this guide, unfortunately now out of print, indispensable for *Apes* collectors.

BOOK AND RECORD SETS

Power Records, 1974, 4 issues
Each of these sets contains a 20-page comic book adaptation of a different *Planet of the Apes* film (*Conquest of the Planet of the Apes*

was the only film not included), and a 45 r.p.m. record that narrates the book's story.

BRITISH ANNUALS
Brown Watson, 1975–77
Hardcover "Annuals" are a tradition in Great Britain. These books based on movies and television shows feature original stories, art, comic strips, text articles, photos, and activity pages. Annuals based on *Planet of the Apes* were released in 1975, 1976, and 1977.

COLORING/ACTIVITY BOOKS
Artcraft, 1974, 6 issues, plus 1 Giant Activity Book
Coloring books with assorted games and quizzes, with illustrated covers depicting scenes from the *Apes* films.

COMIC BOOKS
Beneath the Planet of the Apes
Gold Key, 1970, one issue
The first *Planet of the Apes* comic book was an adaptation of the second *Apes* film. The book featured a photo cover and was packaged with a pull-out poster. The issue was part of Gold Key's *Movie Comics* series, which ran from 1962–1972.

Planet of the Apes
Marvel Comics, 1974–77, 29 issues
Marvel Comics jumped on the Ape-mania bandwagon with a magazine format title, launched in 1974, featuring black-and-white illustrated adaptations of the *Planet of the Apes* films. Originally planned as a bimonthly title, *Planet of the Apes* was upgraded to monthly release after its third issue, a reflection of its immediate popularity. Doug Moench, then a relative newcomer to Marvel, wrote the stories that were illustrated by various artists including Alfredo Alcala, Ed Hannigan, Mike Ploog, and Herb Trimpe and George Tuska. Each magazine also featured *Apes*-related articles and interviews. Legal restrictions forbade the

artists from using the likenesses of Charlton Heston as Taylor, or other actors from the films, but the stories remained fairly close to the original source material. Interestingly, Moench admitted that he never watched the fourth and fifth films prior to adapting them for the magazine. "I'm not even really sure I saw the second one," said Moench in 1999. "I know I didn't bother with the last two."

Adventures on the Planet of the Apes
Marvel Comics, 1975–76, 11 issues
In 1975, Marvel released color reprints of its black and white magazine movie adaptations, in standard comic book form. Since most fans already owned the stories when they were originally published just one year earlier, the *Adventures* series did not prove as popular and was canceled within a year. Of most interest to collectors now are the covers drawn by noted artist Jim Starlin on issues #1 and #6, and by Rich Buckler on #2.

Planet of the Apes Limited Collectors Edition
Adventure Comics, 1990, 4 issues

Planet of the Apes
Adventure Comics, 1990–91, 24 issues

Urchak's Folly
Adventure Comics, 1991, 4 issues

Terror on the Planet of the Apes
Adventure Comics, 1991, 4 issues

Blood of the Apes
Adventure Comics, 1992, 4 issues

Ape City
Adventure Comics, 1990, 4 issues

The Forbidden Zone
Adventure Comics, 1991, 4 issues

Ape Nation
Adventure Comics, 1991, 4 issues

A Day on the Planet of the Apes
Adventure Comics, 1991, 1 issue

Sins of the Father
Adventure Comics, 1992, 1 issue

In 1990, under the creative guidance of writer Charles Marshall, Adventure Comics launched five *Planet of the Apes* titles. The primary series, also titled *Planet of the Apes*, was set one hundred years after the movie *Battle for the Planet of the Apes*, and followed the adventures of Caesar's grandson, Alexander. Other new characters included General Ollo, a gorilla, his mute son Grunt, and Jacob, an orangutan with a similar world view to Dr. Zaius. "The first two films dealt with a planet of the apes in the far future," Marshall told *Comics Scene* magazine in 1990. "I'm trying to set into motion some of the things in the past that will get to that future."

Other series, such as *Ape City*, chronicled the lives of apes in Europe, where the nuclear devastation that destroyed American civilization was not as calamitous. The story chronicles the efforts of Dr. Benday, the smartest ape on earth, to help solve an energy crisis. Society is further threatened by the Baboonjas, a race of Baboon ninja warriors, and the Vindicators, time-traveling killers with superior weapons technology.

Ape Nation was a cross-over series between *Planet of the Apes* and the 1988 film *Alien Nation*, which Charles Marshall wrote.

FANZINES
Apes Chronicles
International *Planet of the Apes* Fan Club, 1991–94, 35 issues

All aspects of *Planet of the Apes* are covered in this fanzine, which features the original comic strip "Veetus" by Jeff Krueger.

Ape Crazy
International *Planet of the Apes* Fan Club, 1993, 7 issues
Photos, comic reviews, commentaries on the *Apes* films and TV shows, and original comic strips by Jerry Brown were featured in this spin-off of *Apes Chronicles*, created by Mark and Tim Wasylyszyn.

NOVELS
Novels Based on the Motion Pictures:
Boulle, Pierre. *Monkey Planet (La Planète Des Singes)* 1963
The book that inspired the movie that inspired a phenomenon, has been out of print for several years in the United States, but a new edition is likely to be released to coincide with the 2001 *Planet of the Apes* film. Three different cover versions were printed, two of which followed the release of the movie in 1967, and feature a photo from the film.

Avallone, Michael. *Beneath the Planet of the Apes.*
Bantam Books, 1970
Michael Avallone's adaptation of the first *Planet of the Apes* sequel follows the film's script, though his portrayal of Brent is arguably more vivid than the one essayed by James Franciscus. The Brent of the novel struggles with the realization that earth is now ruled by intelligent apes, and often seems to teeter on the brink of insanity.

Pournelle, Jerry. *Escape from the Planet of the Apes.*
Award Books, 1971
Paul Dehn's script for the *Escape* film offered no explanation of how a trio of apes from a primitive society could learn how to fly a NASA spaceship, and pilot it back in time to earth in the 20th century. Jerry Pournelle's novel supplies this information, in a

way that is consistent with the movies. At one point, Cornelius tells the federal government commission that his ape society was technologically advanced, but unable to develop technology because of a shortage of fossil fuels.

Jakes, John. *Conquest of the Planet of the Apes.*
Award Books, 1972
Conquest was the most violent of the five *Apes* films, and author John Jakes expands upon this theme, portraying the clash between a militaristic human government and Caesar's ape revolt in even more brutal detail than the PG-rated film could abide. Author John Jakes is more famous now for his novel about another violent uprising, the American Civil War, in *North and South.*

Gerrold, David. *Battle for the Planet of the Apes.*
Award Books, 1973.
David Gerrold was saddled with the unenviable task of adapting the least interesting of the *Apes* films and, despite the addition of several new ideas and situations, he is unable to make the story any more compelling. Gerrold wrote the popular *Star Trek* episode "The Trouble with Tribbles," as well as several well-received novels based on the landmark science-fiction series.

Novels Based on the Television Series:
Effinger, George Alec
Planet of the Apes #1: Man the Fugitive. Award Books, 1975
Planet of the Apes #2: Escape to Tomorrow. Award Books, 1975
Planet of the Apes #3: Journey into Terror. Award Books, 1975
Planet of the Apes #4: Lord of the Apes. Award Books, 1975
George Effinger, a former writer for Marvel Comics (*Gullivar Jones, Warlord of Mars, Creatures on the Loose*), hammered out four novelizations of the short-lived *Planet of the Apes* series, based on original episodes.

Novels Based on Return to the *Planet of the Apes*:

Arrow, William

Visions from Nowhere. Ballantine Books, 1976

Escape from Terror Lagoon. Ballantine Books, 1976

Man, the Hunted Animal. Ballantine Books, 1976

The three novels written by William Arrow cover the entire continuing story featured in 13 episodes of the animated series *Return to the Planet of the Apes.* The story for a 14th episode, "A Date with Judy," was never filmed but has been adapted by Arrow in his third novel, *Man, the Hunted Animal.* Photos from the live-action *Planet of the Apes* series appear on the book covers.

CHAPTER FIVE

THE HISTORY OF *PLANET OF THE APES*
A Timeline

1972

Four astronauts, led by Commander George Taylor, begin a six-month mission in deep space. After their spaceship disappears into a distant future and is presumed lost, a second craft is launched on the same flight path, piloted by Commander Brent. Brent's ship goes Jupiter II as well. (*Planet of the Apes, Beneath the Planet of the Apes*)

1973

Taylor's craft returns to earth, piloted by a trio of chimpanzee scientists named Cornelius, Zira, and Milo. Milo is killed by a gorilla at the Los Angeles Zoo. Cornelius and Zira tell U.S. government officials that their future doesn't look too bright, and are murdered by Dr. Otto Hasslein, a presidential adviser. Their baby son survives. (*Escape from the Planet of the Apes*)

1979

Astronauts Bill Hudson, Jeff Carter, and Judy Franklin blast off in the NASA spacecraft Venturer, in an attempt to test Dr. Stanton's revolutionary theory of "time-thrust." (*Return to the Planet of the Apes*)

1981

Alan Virdon and Peter Burke, who apparently haven't learned anything from other astronauts launched in the same general direction, blast off into space, where their ship encounters an electrical storm near Alpha Centauri and disappears. (*Planet of the Apes* — TV series)

1984

A mysterious space-born plague wipes out the entire dog and cat population on earth. Pet-deprived humans start stocking up on Ape Chow. (*Escape from the Planet of the Apes*)

1991

Caesar, the son of Cornelius and Zira (originally named Milo) accompanies his guardian Armando to a large Western city, to help promote Armando's circus. Caesar protests when he sees an ape being beaten by law enforcement agents, and is nearly apprehended. Armando is arrested. Caesar organizes an ape rebellion, and seizes control of the city. (*Conquest of the Planet of the Apes*)

2001

The world has changed considerably since Caesar's first ape rebellion. Human civilization has been devastated by a nuclear war. Now the leader of a small community of apes and humans, Caesar visits the ruins of San Francisco to view videotapes of his parents. His presence is discovered by a band of warlike mutant humans, who attack Caesar's community. The attack is repelled. Caesar's son, Cornelius, perishes from injuries indirectly caused by General Aldo, a gorilla soldier. (*Battle for the Planet of the Apes*)

2019

An astronaut named Brent, who may or may not be related to the Brent who left earth in 1972, blasts off. The details of his mission are unknown. (*Return to the Planet of the Apes*)

2052

Though relations are tense between humans and apes, some in the species manage to forge friendships. Jason, a human, and Alexander, a chimpanzee, are born. (*Planet of the Apes* — Marvel Comics)

2069

General Brutus, an Ape City peace officer, falls under the control of the Gestalt Mind, one of several factions seeking to rule the world. (Marvel Comics)

2070

The planet gets more screwed up. Jason and Alexander, now 18 years old, battle the Inheritors, a cave-dwelling people based near the Forbidden City. Mutations of apes, men, and a new species somewhere in between battle for dominion over the Forbidden Zone. (Marvel Comics)

3085

Burke and Virdon land with a thud on earth, somewhere near San Francisco. Jones, another astronaut on the ship, does not survive the crash. They are captured and taken to Ape City, where they subsequently escape, accompanied by Galen, a chimpanzee. (*Planet of the Apes* — TV series)

3955

Taylor's spacecraft crash-lands in an inland sea somewhere in the New York City area, though little remains of the Big Apple when the astronauts emerge from their ship. Taylor's crew are killed by the apes, led by Dr. Zaius. Taylor meets Cornelius, Zira, and Nova. He is jailed, tried, and scheduled for nasty medical experiments. Taylor escapes into the Forbidden Zone with Nova, and discovers the half-buried Statue of Liberty. A few months later, Brent's ship lands near Taylor's. He meets Nova, is reunited with Taylor, and battles both gorilla soldiers and a race of telepathic mutants. The planet is destroyed when Taylor detonates the Alpha-Omega bomb. (*Planet of the Apes, Beneath the Planet of the Apes*)

3959

Brent (the second one, not the first one) lands on the ape planet. He is rescued by a band of humans, and nursed back to health by a mute woman, Nova. (*Return to the Planet of the Apes*)

3979

Astronauts Bill Hudson, Jeff Carter, and Judy Franklin land on the ape planet. Apparently, no one told them that it had been blown up 24 years ago. They meet Cornelius, Zira, Dr. Zaius, and, eventually, Brent. They build a fortress for the humans to aid them in their ongoing skirmishes against the apes, led by General Urko. (*Return to the Planet of the Apes*)

CHAPTER SIX

GORILLAS FOR SALE:

Merchandising
Planet of the Apes

Some movies lend themselves better to merchandise tie-ins than others, which is why there aren't any *Sophie's Choice* action figures. Today, it's taken for granted that the release of any animated, science fiction, or fantasy film will be accompanied by a product line, but that was not always the case. The great sci-fi movies of the 1950s and 1960s did not fill toy stores with related merchandise. There were no plastic robots that said "Klaatu, Barada, Nikto" after *The Day the Earth Stood Still* (1951), or assembly-required Martian spacecrafts modeled after those in *War of the Worlds* (1953).

All of that changed with *Planet of the Apes*. But it didn't happen right away. When the film was released in 1967, the only item it inspired was a series of trading cards issued by Topps in 1968. Four *Apes* sequels produced no new merchandise, despite their popularity at the box office.

In 1973, the television network debut of the first film drew a 60 share for CBS. Twentieth Century Fox responded to this audience enthusiasm by bringing all five movies back into theaters. The "Go Ape!" film marathon was a huge success in 1973, and prompted Fox to begin development of an *Apes* television series. At the same time, they investigated the logistics of licensing *Planet of the Apes* merchandise. Pleased with the possibilities, they authorized more than 300 officially licensed items in less than one year.

"The original movie was not aimed at kids," explained Terry Hoknes, President of the International *Planet of the Apes* Fan Club. "The marketing concept created in 1973, after the movies ended, was to promote the TV series to a younger audience. The series died out, but meanwhile tons of merchandise was sold in a very short period of time — possibly six months." In fact, *Apes* action figures, books, and other assorted toys had cash registers ringing to the tune of more than $100 million, an unprecedented amount for movie-related merchandise.

As a result, the influence of *Planet of the Apes* on the marketing of motion pictures cannot be underestimated. Just four years later, *Star Wars* (1977), another Twentieth Century Fox release, took movie merchandising to the next level by promoting items while the film was still in its original release. *Star Wars* items outgrossed even those created by *Planet of the Apes*, and from then on the merchandise tie-in campaign became an integral part of the movie industry.

More than 25 years later, *Planet of the Apes* items remain highly sought-after by fans and collectors. The market, in fact, is as lively now as it's ever been, and should continue to flourish with the release of the 2001 film. A search on the Internet's biggest auction site, eBay, shows more than 700 *Apes* items up for sale in a typical week, with enthusiastic bidding on the rarities. Among the most popular items are the Mego action figures, first released in 1973. Mint on card figures of Alan Virdon, Cornelius, Dr. Zaius, Galen, Pete Burke, and Zira can fetch between $100 and $300 each. An original copy of the *Planet of the Apes* script has sold for $1,500. Most other items routinely sell for less than $100, depending on their condition.

The following list is not comprehensive, and does not include merchandise released to coincide with the 2001 film, or the dozens of unauthorized items produced by various companies during the *Planet of the Apes* "boom" of 1973–1975.

Addar

Model Kits

Caesar, Cornelius, Cornfield Roundup, Dr. Zaius, General Aldo, General Ursus, Gorilla Soldier on horseback, Jailwagon, Treehouse, Zira.

AHI

Action Figures

8" figures of apes in camouflage, and orangutans.

Action Figure Accessories

Friction-Powered Prison Wagon, Helicopter.

Beach Ball

Cycles

"Stunt" and "Zoom" cycles, ridden by Dr. Zaius and Galen.

Parachute Figures

5" plastic figures of Dr. Zaius and Galen, attached to plastic parachutes.

Water Pistols

In figures of Dr. Zaius, Galen, and Cornelius (water shoots through characters' mouths).

Wind-up Figures

Dr. Zaius and Galen in two varieties: walking, and mounted on battery-operated horses.

"Zing Wing" Frisbee

Frisbee in blue and green varieties, with illustration of Dr. Zaius and Galen.

A.J. Renzi
Banks
Monochromatic figures of Cornelius, Dr. Zaius, and General Ursus.

Aladdin
Lunchbox with thermos, depicting images from the *Planet of the Apes* television series.

AOCP
Models made in 1996 by AOCP (Attack of the Clay People): Cornelius, Cornelius in astronaut outfit, Dr. Zaius, Gorilla, Zira.

Aurora
Dr. Zaius and Galen Poster Puzzles, measured nine square feet.

Ben Cooper
Dangle Figures
5" rubber figures of Caesar and a Gorilla Soldier, with string attached to hang figure on rear-view mirror, etc.

Halloween costumes:
Caesar, Dr. Zaius, Galen, Gorilla Warrior, Lisa.

Carnival Toys
17" stuffed dolls of Dr. Zaius and Galen.

Catalog Shoppe
Mix-n-Mold Models
Plastic model casts of Cornelius, Dr. Zaius (two different designs), Galen, General Urko, Peter Burke, and Alan Virdon.

Cheinco

Wastepaper baskets (two styles): round (with Statue of Liberty) and oval (Cornelius, Dr. Zaius, Gorilla Soldier, and Zira on one side, humans in cage on the other).

Chemtoy

"Fun-Doh" Modeling Molds.
Kit with plastic molds of Dr. Zaius, General Aldo, and Zira.

Movie Viewer.

Coleco

Planet of the Apes Playhouse. Five feet tall.

Colorforms

Planet of the Apes Adventure Set, consisting of plastic self-sticking pieces and playboard.

Commonwealth
Dolls

12" dolls, in plush and beanbag varieties, of Dr. Zaius and Galen.

Hand Puppets

Dr. Zaius and Galen.

Cycle Safety

Bike flags, featuring General Aldo, Galen, Dr. Zaius, and Zira.

Deka

Breakfast set featuring bowl, ten-ounce cup, plate, and tumbler, with *Planet of the Apes* logo and various characters. White with red lettering.

Don Post

Masks, composed of rubber and sculpted hair: General Aldo, Cornelius, Dr. Zaius, Gorilla Warrior, Zira.

GAF

Viewmaster reels — Talking and Silent versions. The images on the reel for *Beneath the Planet of the Apes* were believed too violent, so the set was never released. As a result, it is highly sought after by collectors.

H-G Toys

Planet of the Apes archery set, with suction-cup arrows.

Puzzles

Packed in boxes and canisters. Images: Cornelius, Zira, Lucius, General Aldo, General Aldo on Patrol; *Battle for the Planet of the Apes*, and *The Chase*.

Hi-Flyer
Kites

Plastic, with graphics of Ape Head or Gorilla Ape.

Hot Items, Inc.

Dr. Zaius bubble blower.

Ideal
Inflatable dolls

19" tall, three varieties: Dr. Zaius, Galen, General Urko.

Illusive Concepts

Halloween costumes, with sculpted hair, released in 1995: Ape, Gorilla Warrior.

Charlton Heston and his wife are reunited with old friends at the 30th anniversary screening of *Planet of the Apes* (Lisa Rose/ Globe Photos).

Intraptor, Inc.
AM radio, with photo from *Escape from the Planet of the Apes.*

Larami
Billions of Bubbles
Bubble blower.

Boomerangutang
Plastic boomerang.

Chimp-Scope and Gorilla-Scope
Plastic retractable telescopes.

Flashlight
"Monkey Shines" plastic operating flashlight.

Interplanetary Ape-Phone
Set of two Walkie-Talkies with *Planet of the Apes* logo.

Pellet Rifle
Available in blue, brown, and white colors. A plastic gun that fired small, yellow pellets.

Pop N' Spin Pistol and Target Set.

Lee Belt Co.
Bolo ties and belts with colored buckles featuring Alexander, Cornelius, Dr. Zaius, and General Ursus.

Mattel
Rapid Fire Rifle (comes with ape mask)
Tommy Burst Sub-Machine Gun (with ape mask)

Both guns featured the *Planet of the Apes* logo on the barrel.

Matthew Sotis
Action Figures
Series of 8" jointed figures made from 1995 to 1997. Excellent color and detail, and the debut of many characters never before immortalized in plastic, make this set a favorite with fans and collectors: Black Mutant, Conquest Chimpanzee, Conquest Gorilla, Conquest Orangutan, Dodge, Dr. Honorius, Dr. Zaius, Fatman Mutant, Female Gorilla, General Urko, General Ursus in Steambath, Gorilla Sergeant, Julius, Landon, Mutant Mendez, Taylor.

Action Figure Accessories
General Urko Custom Headquarters.

Masks
Made from actual makeup molds used on the *Planet of the Apes* films: Caesar, Dr. Zaius, Gorilla Warrior, Mutant, Zira.

Mego
Action Figures, 8" tall, posable
Astronaut, Peter Burke, Cornelius, Dr. Zaius, Galen, Soldier Ape, Alan Virdon, General Urko, General Ursus, Zira.

Action Figure Accessories
Battering Ram, Catapult and Wagon, Forbidden Zone Trap Playset, Fortress Playset, Jail, Dr. Zaius Throne, Treehouse Playset, Village Playset.

Bendies
Flexible figures of Astronaut, Cornelius, Dr. Zaius, Galen, Soldier Ape, Zira. Special display box also produced.

Stickers
Set of five, in two styles, small (under 2") and large (7").

Vending Machine Necklaces
Five different heads from Mego action figures (Astronaut,

Cornelius, Dr. Zaius, Gorilla Soldier, and Zira), marketed in amusement machines as necklace medallions.

Milton Bradley
Planet of the Apes board game.

Noble & Cooley
Planet of the Apes drum set.

Our Way
62" cardboard jointed figure of Galen.

P. Moreno
"Apejoe"(G.I. Joe-style) figures, manufactured in 1996: Cornelius, Dr. Zaius, General Aldo, General Ursus, Julius, Mutant Human, Taylor, Zira.

Phoenix
Candy boxes
Eight different styles, contained candy and two prizes.

The Planet Company
In 1994, The Planet Company of Beverly Hills purchased a selection of actual costumes worn in the *Planet of the Apes* films from collector Fuller French, and offered them for sale to the public at $2,995. Orangutan, chimpanzee, and gorilla suits were available.

PLAY PAL
Banks
Two models, Dr. Zaius and Galen. Both figures are depicted standing, and are more colorful and detailed in appearance than the A.J. Renzi banks.

Pressman
Planet of the Apes Quick Draw Cartoons, Ring Toss Game, and Spin'N'Color Game.

Rainbow Card Company
Planet of the Apes Archive Premium Trading Card Set
1997 release of 90 cards, featuring images from all five *Apes* films. Some packs contained autographed insert cards of Nova, Lisa, Caspay, Ongaro, and Julius.

Resinator
Busts of Cornelius, Dr. Zaius, Gorilla. Manufactured in 1995.

Saalfield
Planet of the Apes magic slate.

Stan Lee
Rings, with display box, made in Great Britain.

Topps, Inc.
Trading Cards
Two series, one from the film *Planet of the Apes*, and one from the *Apes* television series. The 44-card movie set was released in 1968, making it the only *Planet of the Apes* collectible that coincided with the film's original release. The TV series set featured 66 cards. Display boxes were made with each set.

Well-Made Toys
Action Figures
9" and 12" plush toy figures of Dr. Zaius and Galen. Also made in "dangle" variety.

Whitman
Puzzles
Images: General Urko and Soldier, General Urko and Burke; General Urko and Dr. Zaius; Caesar, Virgil, and Lisa.

Winner Promotions
Planet of the Apes Stain Glass Craft Kit.

CHAPTER SEVEN

GOING APE!
The *Planet of the Apes* Superfans

Fans. Almost every movie has them, even the ones Paulie Shore makes. But there's something about the science fiction genre that attracts a special kind of devotion among small groups of fans, who inevitably find each other and share their enthusiasm in clubs and conventions.

The landmark television series *Star Trek* (1966–69) is recognized as the first sci-fi enterprise (no pun intended) to attract an organized cult following, but *Planet of the Apes* deserves equal credit, as the first film series to inspire an international fellowship of admirers. In both cases, the ground swell of interest was a delayed reaction; the Trekkers didn't really get organized until after the series was canceled in 1969. *Planet of the Apes* fans, who as yet have no designation (Apesters? Ape-pees?), first banded together in the early 1970s when the television series premiered, the movies were re-released into theaters, and *Apes* merchandise filled an aisle in Toys 'R' Us.

Here, in their own words, are the stories of four such fans.

Jeff Krueger and Natalie Trundy at Point Dune, California, the setting for the climactic finale of *Planet of the Apes* (Courtesy Jeff Krueger).

TERRY HOKNES

Saskatoon, Saskatchewan, Canada
President, International Planet of the Apes Fan Club

WHY *APES*?

I was a big sci-fi nut, who grew up on *Star Wars*. I like stuff with imagination, but I guess it was the sensitive part of me that really took up with *Planet of the Apes*, and the issue of racial prejudice. The film series has always made me think, and I was intrigued by the fact that the whole concept seemed plausible.

WHEN DID YOU BECOME A FAN?

I was born in 1971, and missed the original release of the movies and the initial merchandise hype around the TV series. When I was in first grade, I saw some of *Planet of the Apes* on television for the first time, but didn't really pay attention. But in 1982, when I was 11, they showed all five movies on TV late at night, and for some reason I just had to watch them. Then in 1986, my tenth grade English teacher decided to show the first film in class, hoping it would "get us thinking." I was very sick that week and skipped school every day, but I would show up in the afternoons just for that class to catch the film, and hear the students talk about it. It was at that point that I realized these movies were special to me.

ANY FAVORITES?

I'm now hooked on the live action and the cartoon series. I think they're both underrated, which makes me like them even more than the original films.

FAVORITE CHARACTERS?

I have always said that my favorite is the Lawgiver; the whole series revolves around the rules and mysteries of his character. Dr.

Zaius is intriguing also. Zira is just a plain fun character and I would rate her highly as well. Surprisingly, the human characters like Taylor and Nova don't excite me as much, though of course their importance to the stories is not to be underestimated.

DO YOU COLLECT *APES*?

I started buying the original comic books and the movies around 1987. The comics were worth almost nothing at the time, but my local comic shops never had any of them. Now, I have about 50 copies of all the *Planet of the Apes* magazines and comic books. I sell and trade some with other fans, but I always keep a high-grade copy of every comic, magazine, and paperback printed in the U.S. I also have a rare, complete collection of all 139 *Planet of the Apes* weekly comics that were printed in the United Kingdom in the 1970s, as well as one of the largest collections anywhere of foreign language Apes comics, including items from Finland and Germany.

I never got too heavily into the toys and other items. They are tough to find and you have to pay a fortune to get them.

HIGHLIGHTS OF THE COLLECTION?

There were three comics released by Marvel in 1976 under the title *Adventures on the Planet of the Apes*. There were 11 issues in the series, but Marvel did a test print run of issues 5–7 with a higher price tag on the covers. They were sent out to only a few major U.S. cities, and are nearly impossible to find now. I have all three, and have been told there may be less than ten copies of each in existence.

The *Lord of the Apes #4* paperback is also difficult to track down. I have purchased only four copies in the last 15 years.

HOW DID THE INTERNATIONAL
PLANET OF THE APES FAN CLUB BEGIN?

In 1990 Adventure Comics started a new line of comics based on the *Planet of the Apes* series. I had four letters published in those books, including one about finding a fan club. But there wasn't any, so I decided to start one in 1991. Though the club still isn't very large, our Web site has had more than 27,000 visitors, and we have members in ten different countries.

Ape Chronicles is the name I came up with for our fanzine. Each issue features articles on the movies, TV series, cartoons, the actors, and behind-the-scenes crew, plus original stories and artwork, interviews, reviews, merchandise information, items for sale, and the "Ape Encyclopedia," which is an in-depth look at every aspect of the mythos. We've even published unused scripts from the series and the films.

FAVORITE TOPIC OF CONVERSATION
AMONG *APES* FANS?

Continuity is very important to many serious fans, including myself. We've devoted many articles in the fanzine to this topic, and will continue to do so. Even though it's a far-fetched science fiction story, we still like to try and make it all "fit" together. Many fans don't like the original stories in the comics because they sometimes break away from continuity. The comics vary from good to ridiculously funny, but I do believe that the one-shot "Sins of the Father" comic is an amazing story that tries to tie in missing facts from the original film.

Natalie Trundy (left), who appeared in four of the five *Planet of the Apes* films, meets her fans of all species (Courtesy Jeff Krueger).

KEN TAYLOR
Sydney, Australia

WHY *APES*?

I remember being impressed by the makeup (as I've always been a fan of monsters and monster makeup), the costumes, and the art direction (although at the age of 12, I had no idea what art direction was). I just thought the whole concept was cool and exciting.

WHEN DID YOU BECOME A FAN?

My first exposure to the *Apes* saga was when the first movie aired on TV in Australia in February of 1975, as a precursor to the premiere of the TV series. I was hooked from that moment on, and watched all 14 episodes religiously, and I eagerly awaited each airing of the movie sequels. I was devastated when the show was unceremoniously replaced by *Space 1999*.

FAVORITE CHARACTERS?

My favorite characters are Zira and Cornelius. I just love them in *Escape*, even though it has a tragic *Romeo and Juliet* ending. My favorite actor has to be Roddy McDowall. He brought so much humanity to each of the different characters he played. For me, he *is Planet of the Apes*. My other favorite character is General Ursus from *Beneath*, because of the performance of James Gregory. He epitomized the warmonger gorilla perfectly.

DO YOU COLLECT?

I had some items when I was a kid, such as the Mego figures, model kits, gum cards, and magazines. Later, I put my *Apes* fanaticism to one side while I pursued other interests (i.e., girls), and gave most of my collection away. I started collecting again seven years ago, and now have over 300 items.

ANY FAVORITE ITEMS?

Surprisingly, most of my favorite items are among the most common: the Mego dolls (for nostalgia value), Don Post masks, Addar Model Kits, Aladdin Lunch Box, and the recently released set of three tin figural wind-ups from Medicom in Japan. Some of the rarest items I have include the set of two figural head water guns mint on card, the set of three inflatable 24-inch figures from Ideal (still in original packaging), a set of fuzzy "Playfeet" slippers still packaged, and an example of each species' original facial appliance which includes a male chimp, female chimp (believed to be Natalie Trundy's from *Battle*), a male gorilla and male orangutan. It's amazing what some collectors will pay for an item when caught up in the eBay auction frenzy. I learned to become patient as many items thought to be "Holy Grails" have in fact appeared numerous times.

WHAT IS IT ABOUT *PLANET OF THE APES* THAT STILL SPEAKS TO PEOPLE NOW?

It's a classic story: Man's demise at his own hand. That's a theme that is just as pertinent today as it was back then.

ANTHONY R. JAMES
"The Apeman"
Salem, Oregon

"THE APEMAN?"

I picked up that nickname on the Internet, and then when other people found out about my being a fan of *Planet of the Apes*, the name just stuck.

WHEN DID YOU BECOME A FAN?

I first discovered *Planet of the Apes* when I was ten years old, and saw the TV series. Wow, what a cool show! I do not remember even seeing the movies as a kid. Most of my interest was in the show, which I still enjoy more. Recently I obtained every episode on tape, and still watch them regularly.

FAVORITE CHARACTER?

General Urko is my ultimate favorite. I have always been a big fan of the larger than life characters, from Gene Simmons in *Kiss* to Darth Maul and Darth Vader in *Star Wars*. Urko fits into that category — big character, big build, big helmet, and big army of gorilla soldiers.

DO YOU COLLECT?

Back in 1996 I wasn't hooked into the Internet so I wasn't able to find any *Ape* dolls or *Ape* toys anywhere. I checked all the antique stores and even toy shows, to no avail. Then I met eBay, and I went nuts. Thousands of dollars later I had quite a collection. My favorite toy is the lunch box, followed by the Mego action figure of General Urko.

FAVORITE *APES* MEMORY?

I went to the *Planet of the Apes* 30th anniversary show in Los Angeles, and met Linda Harrison, Booth Colman, Buck Kartalian, Lee Delano, Don Pedro Colley, and Ron Harper (to me the coolest guy there), who played Alan Virdon on the TV series. I had some TV series T-shirts made and brought some to the show. I gave Ron one and he wore it the next day, and let me sit at his table and talk to him in between autographs.

JEFF KRUEGER
West Hollywood, California

WHEN DID YOU BECOME A FAN?

My first look was a CBS network showing of *Escape from the Planet of the Apes*, either its broadcast premiere or the repeat, sometime in the 1973–74 season. I remember having seen a commercial, I think for *Battle*, so I was familiar with the signature makeup enough to register a shock of recognition when the chimps take off their helmets. That moment is seared into my memory. My babysitter had turned it on and I didn't know it was playing that

Superfan Jeff Krueger and friend (Courtesy Jeff Krueger).

night. I just remember I was occupied with something else and that moment came and I was glued to the TV. It was an inauspicious beginning because I fell asleep and missed the ending. But while I was awake I was fascinated and thus began a lifelong passion. I was nine years old. Soon after my first viewing of *Escape*, the original run of the TV series began and that's what hooked me.

WHY *APES*?

The thing that comes to mind is the makeup (what a classic look) and the unique story. But I'm sure even back then there was more to it than that. Now I know about history, religion, the ways of culture, etc. I don't think my ape-preciation is greater than when I was a kid, but it has deepened. It certainly stayed with me even after science fiction movies became more visually elaborate (I remember being jealous that *Star Wars* received so much attention while *Apes* languished). And *Escape* remains my favorite *Apes* sequel, a close second to the original.

FAVORITE CHARACTERS?

Well, I'm good friends with Natalie Trundy, so I guess she's the sentimental favorite. I've always enjoyed her predecessor in the female ape makeup, Kim Hunter. Zira was a very touching portrayal. She was a strong female sci-fi character long before Ripley and Princess Leia. Of course, any character Roddy McDowall played is worthy. Armando (Ricardo Montalban) is also a favorite because to me he is the heart of the middle of the series. I also liked the TV characters, especially Urko and the astronauts.

DO YOU COLLECT?

In the Fall of 1974 I was particularly taken with the Mego action figures and the trash can. Christmas 1974 was definitely a *Planet of the Apes* Christmas. I soon busted my Mego figures (since they were only held together by those damn strings) and spent the next 15 years looking for replacements. During the 1990s I was able to get most of them, though the prices weren't kids' stuff. Or maybe they were. Many kids today are even more ruthless as collectors than their elders and seem to have lost the fun of toys.

I had some *Apes* stuff as a kid. None of it lasted long and it wasn't until 1982 that I started gathering it again. I picked up the

Jeff Krueger visits the beach where Taylor battled the forces of Dr. Zaius (Courtesy Jeff Krueger).

odd item, the Marvel mags (which I didn't know about as a kid), other paperbacks. In 1988, a friend of mine was crazy about Batman, who was about to get a pop culture facelift (ironically, from a Tim Burton movie) and I started going to a few sci-fi conventions with him. Seeing old *Apes* stuff brought back fond memories and I slowly started picking stuff up: the trading cards, posters, nothing extravagant. In 1990, the new comics hit and that really ignited the flame. Not that they were great (though I liked them), but it was *Planet of the Apes* brought up to date. Suddenly the concept was now, it wasn't something in the past. Eventually I was able to build up a collection of my beloved Megos, an interesting collection of *Ape*-related magazines and various odds and ends. I think my collection is modest but to outsiders it might seem extreme.

ANY FAVORITE ITEMS?

My favorite is an autographed copy of Eric Greene's book *Planet of the Apes As American Myth*, signed by many of the principals, among them Chuck Heston, Roddy McDowall, Kim Hunter, Natalie Trundy, Linda Harrison, John Chambers, James Cameron, Jane Goodall, the babysitter who introduced me to *Apes*, and many more (and many yet to come).

FAVORITE *APES* MEMORY?

I was the first person who joined the International *Planet of the Apes* Fan Club (after founder Terry Hoknes). I learned about the fan club from the new comic books and thought it would be a fun idea. Through the club I was put in contact with people who in turn hooked me up with some incredible events. The highlight thus far was being invited as a journalist to the 30th Anniversary *Apes* party in 1998, seeing a new print of the movie, and hanging with the stars and creators. What more could a fan ask for?

WHAT IS IT ABOUT *PLANET OF THE APES* THAT STILL SPEAKS TO PEOPLE NOW?

Obviously the great visuals have been surpassed so it's not that (though I think *Apes* has a unique look that hasn't dated). I think it's the humanity of the concept and the ideals it encompasses. We get such a hard sell in pop culture, everything is whitewashed and market researched to death. I think it's refreshing to see something that sticks to its guns and doesn't cop out with a "happy ending." Beyond that the time flopping of the series is fascinating; they are solid adventures, well told and acted. Hype fades, quality endures. What's interesting about the sequels is that they're each a different kind of storytelling. The original is a solid science-fiction adventure, *Beneath* is an epic diatribe, *Escape* is a chamber drama, *Conquest* is a political allegory, and *Battle* is a vengeance story. And each has a different look, different strengths and weaknesses. It goes against the usual sequel wisdom of "more of the same." Something for everyone.

CHAPTER EIGHT

PLANET OF THE APES:

References/Spoofs/Tributes

Like *Superman*, *Star Trek*, and *Star Wars*, the story and characters of *Planet of the Apes* are now a permanent part of our popular culture. Writers of films and TV shows from all genres have used *Apes* references in their projects, confident that most of the audience will get the joke.

MOVIES:

Austin Powers: The Spy Who Shagged Me (1999)

When swinging secret agent Austin Powers (Mike Myers) travels back in time to the 1960s, Felicity Shagwell (Heather Graham) asks him what the future is like. Replies Austin, "Well, everyone has a flying car, entire meals come in pill form, and the earth is ruled by damn dirty apes!"

Bleeder (1999)

A disturbing but riveting Danish film that paints a bleak portrait of contemporary society, *Bleeder* stars Kim Bodnia as Leo, who cannot deal rationally with his wife's pregnancy. His only escape from an unhappy reality is a weekly "schlock movie" night with his friends. One of the titles they rent is *Planet of the Apes*.

Free Enterprise (1998)

Underrated, often hilarious study of two obsessed *Star Trek* and science fiction fans, Robert (Rafer Weigel) and Mark (Eric McCormack), who meet their idol, William Shatner (who plays himself). In one typically amusing scene, Robert uses as a pick-up line: "I have the Japanese import box set of all five *Planet of the Apes* films on laserdisc — letterboxed." And it works! Later, during a discussion of favorite sexual fantasy actresses, Mark nominates Linda Harrison as Nova: "She's the perfect woman — gorgeous, scantily-clad . . . mute."

Krippendorf's Tribe (1998)

A hit-and-miss comedy about an anthropologist who invents a lost tribe in New Guinea after spending all his university grant money on his family. Late in the film, Mickey (Gregory Smith), the oldest son of Professor James Krippendorf (Richard Dreyfuss), wears a *Planet of the Apes* T-shirt.

20 Dates (1998)

Early in this film documentary of his love life, narrator/star Myles Berkowitz talks about how he didn't need a big budget for his first movie, while scenes from more expensive films, including *Planet of the Apes*, play on screen. We see the scene where Taylor and Zira kiss, an appropriate choice for a movie about complex relationships.

Eight Days a Week (1997)

A weak comedy with a clever premise — a nerdy boy (Josh Schaefer) in love with his beautiful neighbor (Keri Russell) decides to camp out on her front lawn until she succumbs to his charms. Late in his campaign for romance, however, he laments that he's "stranded in the 'Friend' zone, like Charlton Heston being marooned in *Planet of the Apes*."

George of the Jungle (1997)
Spoiled rich boy Lyle (Thomas Haden Church) makes fun of the jungle legend of a white ape, suggesting he probably runs the candy counter at the Bujumbura cineplex where *Planet of the Apes* is playing on all 14 screens.

Rocketman (1997)
Kids will love this zany slapstick comedy, featuring Harland Williams as Fred Z. Randall, a computer geek who becomes a last-minute substitute astronaut. During his first visit to NASA, Randall meets a chimpanzee living in a Gaudi-esque habitat modeled on *Planet of the Apes*. He calls the chimp "little Dr. Zaius."

Mother (1996)
When writer John Henderson (Albert Brooks) moves back in with his mother (Debbie Reynolds), he hangs a *Planet of the Apes* movie poster on the wall of his old room.

Spy Hard (1996)
Leslie Nielsen stars as Agent Dick Steele in this James Bond spoof. When the villains attempt to strap Steele's partner, Agent Barbara Dahl (Stephanie Romanov), to a missile, she yells, "Get your stinking paws off me, you damn dirty ape!"

Dunston Checks In (1996)
Dunston, a friendly orangutan, is left to watch television in a luxury hotel room by his larcenous owner (Rupert Everett). He channel-surfs past various programs, and stops on the scene from *Planet of the Apes* where Zira kisses Taylor.

The Best Movie Ever Made (1994)
The title of this sketch comedy film is woefully inaccurate, but *Planet of the Apes* fans might enjoy a recurring skit called "Battle for the Planet of Cheese," which sends up *Apes*, *Star Wars*, and other science-fiction classics.

The Chase (1994)

Escaped convict Jack Hammond (Charlie Sheen) is chased by what seems like every cop in America in this diverting action film. Late in the chase, a policeman is watching television and catches the "damn dirty ape" line from Charlton Heston in the first film. Another guy watching in the room says, "Hey, cool, monkeys!"

Reality Bites (1994)

In this sparkling slacker comedy, television executive Michael (Ben Stiller) has a statue of Dr. Zaius on his desk, which is broken by Lelaina (Winona Ryder). She tries to put it back together, until Michael somberly announces, "I think he's gone."

Do the Right Thing (1989)

Pizza shop worker Pino (John Turturro) utters the thinly-veiled racial epithet "Every day I come to work, it's like *Planet of the Apes*" in Spike Lee's emotionally-charged drama.

Hell Comes to Frogtown (1987)

The opening scene of this post-apocalyptic story, pitting the last humans on earth against giant mutated frogs, features the Statue of Liberty standing in a deserted wasteland. Wrestler Roddy Piper plays Sam Hell, who battles Commander Toady, who no one will confuse with General Urko.

Spaceballs (1987)

Although this Mel Brooks comedy is primarily a send-up of the *Star Wars* trilogy, other films are also lampooned, including *Planet of the Apes*. Watch the scene where a mutating monster spaceship takes the form of a giant metallic chambermaid holding a vacuum. When the ship is destroyed, the head and the arm of the chambermaid land on a desert planet, in a way that resembles the Statue of Liberty. The scene fades out as two chimpanzees ride toward the ship on horseback.

Time of the Apes (1987)

A blatant ripoff of *Planet of the Apes*, this low-budget production was compiled from several episodes of a Japanese television series. A mother takes her two children to visit their uncle, a scientist studying cryogenics. During an earthquake, the family is sealed in cryogenic chambers, and wakes up in a distant future when apes rule the earth. *Time of the Apes* can be seen in reruns of *Mystery Science Theater 3000*.

Spaceship (1981)

Inept spoof of the science fiction genre, made in Canada with a budget of about ten dollars. But with a cast including Leslie Nielsen, Patrick Macnee, and Cindy Williams, it almost qualifies for "so bad it's good" status. At one point Williams is watching "Earth News" on a monitor, and sees footage of a gorilla soldier invasion.

Aysecik ve Sihirli Cüceler Rüyalar Ülkesinde (1971)

Made in Turkey, this adaptation of *The Wizard of Oz* features two subtle, indirect references to *Planet of the Apes*. When the Winkies, loyal to the witch, capture the Cowardly Lion and tear apart the Scarecrow and Tin Woodsman, the set is very similar to the rock formations in *Apes*, and the shot sequence is virtually identical to shots in the first *Apes* film.

MUSIC:

They Might Be Giants
"Severe Tire Damage" (1998)
The group They Might Be Giants slipped seven hidden tracks on their "Severe Tire Damage" CD, all inspired by *Planet of the Apes*. The songs, largely improvised in the studio, are "Planet of the Apes," "Return of the Planet of the Apes," "Conquest of the Planet

of the Apes," "Escape from the Planet of the Apes," "Battle for the Planet of the Apes," "Beneath the Planet of the Apes," and "This Ape's for You."

Blak Twang
"Real Estate" (1996)
British rap group Blak Twang sang "My estate is like *Planet of the Apes*, where puffy jackets with hoods replace the black capes."

TELEVISION:

Serta mattress commercial (1999)
In the surreal world of dreams, according to this commercial's velvet-voiced narrator, it is possible to have afternoon tea with your high school sweetheart, and Cornelius from *Planet of the Apes*.

Seinfeld (January 15, 1998)
In "The Reverse Peephole" (#160) Elaine (Julia Louis-Dreyfuss) sees her boyfriend David Puddy (Patrick Warburton) in a full-length fur coat, and refers to him as Dr. Zaius. In an earlier episode, "The Cafe" (#25), Elaine tries to explain to George (Jason Alexander) how busy the cafe was that day and Jerry throws his arms in the air shouting, "It's a madhouse!"

Buffy the Vampire Slayer (September 15, 1997)
The series' second-season opener, "When She Was Bad," features Xander (Nicholas Brendan) quoting Charlton Heston: "It's a madhouse! A mad . . ."; his friend Willow (Alyson Hannigan) picks up on the reference. "*Planet of the Apes!*"

Mystery Science Theater 3000 (1997)
There have been no shortage of *Apes* references during the film commentary by Mike and the robots on this terrific cult show.

But in February of 1997, everybody's favorite spaceship-bound robots began an ongoing *Apes* spoof featuring Kevin Murphy as the chimp Bobo, Mike Nelson as Dr. Peanut, and Mary Jo Pehl as the Lawgiver.

Eek, the Cat (1996)

Film and television parodies are a specialty of this Saturday morning cartoon series about Eek, a purple kitty. Episode titles include "The Good, the Bad, and the Squishy," "Chariots of Fur," and "The Eeks Files." In "Planet of the Crêpes," an astronaut named Taylor (who has a passing resemblance to Charlton Heston) travels back in time to find dinosaurs, and meets series regulars Bill and Scooter.

The Simpsons (March 24, 1996)

Several episodes of *The Simpsons* feature *Planet of the Apes* references. "The Itchy and Scratchy Show" once did an episode entitled "Planet of the Aches." Reverend Lovejoy referenced *Conquest of the Planet of the Apes* in one of his sermons. Background music from the *Apes* score was used in a scene featuring the children of Springfield being rounded up in a cornfield. And in "Deep Space Homer," Homer becomes an astronaut and worried that he'll be sent to "that terrible Planet of the Apes." But the most comprehensive and entertaining *Apes* spoof ever mounted, on *The Simpsons* or anywhere else, was the 1996 episode "A Fish Called Selma," which featured the musical opus "Stop the Planet of the Apes, I Want to Get Off!" Sample lyric: "I hate every ape I see, from chimpan-A to chimpan-Z."

By Dawn's Early Light (HBO, 1990)

In this Cold War thriller based on William Prochnau's *Trinity's Child*, an accidental U.S. missile attack on Russia nearly starts World War III. As tensions mount on both sides, the co-pilot of a nuclear bomber asks the pilot, "What will happen if this gets out of hand?" The pilot responds, "*Planet of the Apes*, baby!"

Saturday Night Live (March 28, 1987)

When Charlton Heston hosted *Saturday Night Live*, the show opened with Heston falling asleep in the green room, and awakening to discover that the entire cast had turned into apes.

That's Hollywood (1976–1982)

Hosted by Tom Bosley, this syndicated half-hour series was a spin-off of the film *That's Entertainment* (1974). Each show, packed with clips from various Twentieth Century Fox films, was built around a specific theme; one program was devoted to *Planet of the Apes*.

Lost in Space (October 19, 1966)

Many *Planet of the Apes* fans believe that the episode "Prisoners of Space" features experimental ape makeup on a race of aliens encountered by the Robinson family. There has been no acknowledgment of any connection by John Chambers, and the episode was not mentioned in the documentary *Behind the Planet of the Apes*. But the similarities cannot be denied.

MAGAZINES:

Cinefantastique (Summer, 1972)

The sci-fi magazine devoted a special issue to *Planet of the Apes*.

Cracked #123 (March, 1975)

"We monkey around with the apes!" boasted this *Mad*-like parody magazine of its cover story.

Mad #157 (March, 1973)

"The Milking of the Planet That Went Ape" was the title of *Mad*'s cover story.

Entertainment Weekly (October, 1998)

When the list-happy entertainment magazine cataloged the 100 all-time greatest works of science fiction, *Planet of the Apes* ranked #17.

CHAPTER NINE

THERE'S NO BUSINESS LIKE MONKEY BUSINESS

Hollywood has always been an ape-friendly town. Let's face it, show business is one of the few fields left where less highly-evolved creatures can still make a good living. Cornelius and Dr. Zaius you already know about, so here's a list of other simian superstars from film and television.

AT THE MOVIES:

Dunston Checks In (Twentieth Century Fox, 1996)

Take one luxury hotel, add a flustered concierge (Jason Alexander), a Leona Helmsley-esque businesswoman (Faye Dunaway), a suave jewel thief (Rupert Everett), two precocious kids, and one larcenous orangutan, and you've got all the ingredients necessary for screwball comedy. *Dunston Checks In* boasts a cast of A-list players that you don't expect to see feeding straight lines to a monkey, and that's a big part of its appeal.

Ed (Universal, 1996)

Apparently, 1996 was a big year for monkey movies. In *Ed*, Matt LeBlanc plays minor-league scrub Jack "Deuce" Cooper, who finds it hard to adjust to his new teammate and roommate — a talented chimp named Ed. The movie doesn't rise to the same level of mediocrity as *Dunston Checks In*, but it might be more enjoyable for the under-10 crowd because of the baseball storyline and the performance of Matt LeBlanc (kids always like it when they know they're smarter than the actor on screen).

Monkey Shines (Orion, 1988)

In this underrated horror film, written and directed by George Romero, a paralyzed college student receives a monkey named Ella from one of his professors. Ella has been trained to assist the handicapped with everyday tasks, but the student soon discovers that Ella has other talents — among them acting upon her owner's repressed fury at the people who have wronged him. *Monkey Shines* delivers the necessary horror jolts, but it's also a powerful psychological thriller that asks provocative questions about what it means to be human.

Every Which Way But Loose (Warner Bros., 1978)

It's not easy to steal a movie from Clint Eastwood, but an orangutan named Clyde did it twice. In *Every Which Way But Loose* and its 1980 sequel, *Any Which Way You Can*, Clyde's comedic antics overshadow Eastwood's laconic performance as trucker and bare-knuckles fighting champ Philo Beddoe. Some of Clyde's reactions are almost human, and as an actor he's a lot more talented than costar Sondra Locke.

Jungle Book (Disney, 1967)

In Disney's delightful animated version of Rudyard Kipling's story, King Louis is one cool be-boppin' orangutan, thanks to the voice provided by jazz vocalist Louis Prima. Though Baloo the

Bear's "The Bare Necessities" earned the Oscar nomination for Best Song, it's Prima's showstopping "I Wanna Be Like You" that most viewers will be humming after the picture ends.

Robot Monster (1953)

Universally heralded as one of the worst movies ever made, *Robot Monster* tells the frightening tale of earth's invasion by "Earth Ro-Man," a killer robot from Mars. Unfortunately, producer-director Phil Tucker's budget came up a little short when it was time to create the "terrifying" alien invader, so he improvised by costuming his creature in a gorilla suit and deep-sea diving helmet. You've gotta see it to believe it.

Bedtime for Bonzo (Universal, 1951)

Democrats love to ridicule Ronald Reagan's film career, and many of their best barbs are reserved for this domestic comedy in which Reagan, as Professor Peter Boyd, becomes a surrogate parent to a chimp named Bonzo. Once you get past the political critiques, however, what's left is a charming family film, featuring a typically good-natured performance from Reagan. Kids will love Bonzo, one of the most expressive and energetic movie monkeys. The sequel, *Bonzo Goes to College* (1952), is also worth a look.

Mighty Joe Young (RKO, 1949)

In 1949, RKO Pictures tried to revive King Kong-mania by introducing another oversized gorilla. Mighty Joe Young is found in Africa and brought to the U.S. to appear in a nightclub act, but goes on a rampage after the customers feed him too many cocktails. The Ray Harryhausen special effects are still impressive, but the film can't shake its been-there, done-that feeling. A 1998 remake, costarring charming Charlize Theron, had a better sense of humor.

The Ape Man (**Monogram, 1943**)

Bela Lugosi plays the slightly unbalanced Dr. Brewster, who consumes a secret potion and begins to transform into an ape. With the help of his assistant, an actual gorilla, Brewster kills people to drain their spinal fluid (yuck), which he believes will reverse the transformation. *The Ape Man* is proof that Lugosi was capable of making awful horror films long before he met Ed Wood.

King Kong (RKO, 1933)

The granddaddy of all ape movies, and a revered motion picture classic, the original *King Kong* can still move an audience to chills, cheers, and even tears. There's movie magic in every frame in Kong's first appearance on Skull Island, his romance with Fay Wray, and his ascension of the Empire State Building. If you haven't seen it yet, put down this book and go rent it. Like *Planet of the Apes*, *King Kong* has been dissected and analyzed for deeper sociological meaning, but it is first and foremost a creature feature, and maybe the best one ever made.

The same can't be said for the 1976 remake, produced by Dino De Laurentiis at a cost of $20 million. After a big (and undeniably effective) build-up to Kong's first appearance, audiences suppressed a collective chuckle when all they saw was a guy in a bad gorilla suit. Worth seeing anyway, though, for the screen debut of Jessica Lange, who spends most of the movie in clothes that are either see-through or shredded.

Tarzan, the Ape Man (MGM, 1932)

There have been more movies made about Tarzan than any other character from history or fiction. The jungle king, created by Edgar Rice Burroughs, has been featured in more than 50 films, from the silent era through Disney's 1999 animated adaptation. The most popular movie Tarzan was played by Johnny Weissmuller, who appeared in 12 films, often alongside his faithful chimpanzee friend, Cheta. One of the smarter movie chimps, Cheta often helped Tarzan in his adventures, and even fired a tommy gun at Nazi troops in 1943's *Tarzan Triumphs*. Other screen Tarzans, including Herman Brix and Gordon Scott, also had their Chetas; Mike Henry opted for another chimp named Dinky, who bit him on the set of *Tarzan and the Valley of Gold* (1966). Serves them right.

ON TV:

Chimp Channel (TBS, 1999–)

In 1999, the TBS network began airing 2–3 minute parodies of hit movies, featuring chimpanzees in the lead roles. These popular spoofs evolved into the Chimp Channel, which now sends up television shows as well with titles like *NYPD Zoo*, *Treewatch*, and *Ally McSqueal*.

Friends (NBC, 1994–)

Three guys, three girls, and a spider monkey. For the first few seasons of this must-see TV sitcom staple, Ross Geller (David Schwimmer) owned a pet monkey named Marcel, who stole several scenes from his costars while making 1/1000th of their salary. Maybe that's why he's not around anymore. Demonstrating his versatility, Marcel effortlessly shifted from comedy to drama when he costarred with Dustin Hoffman as the plague-carrying monkey in the 1995 feature *Outbreak*.

BJ and the Bear (NBC, 1979–81)

Critics called this a ripoff of the CBS hit *The Dukes of Hazzard*. If I were the Dukes I'd be insulted, since *BJ and the Bear* had two stars, and one of them was a monkey. Greg Evigan played BJ (Billie Joe) McCay, a happy-go-lucky trucker who traveled America's highways with his pet chimp, Bear. Their nemesis was Sheriff Elroy Lobo (Claude Akins) who proved popular enough to inspire a spinoff series.

The Great Grape Ape Show (ABC, 1977–78)

Not one of the more celebrated creatures from the Hanna-Barbera menagerie, but if you've ever seen it, the visual sticks with you — a 30-foot tall purple gorilla, dressed in a green vest, bow tie, and beanie, riding on the roof of a van, and referring to himself in the third person in a voice that sounded like a beer belch. Grape Ape (voiced by Bob Holt) and his friend Beegle Beagle spent most of their time just trying to keep out of trouble, usually without success. The character was revived on *Scooby's All-Star Laff-a-Lympics*, and even had his own board game, but once the 1970s ended, the Grape Ape cult ran out of juice.

Me and the Chimp (CBS, 1972)

Dentist Mike Reynolds (Ted Bessell) found his household turned upside down when his two kids brought home a chimp named Buttons. This short-lived sitcom consisted of little more than Buttons mugging for the camera and turning on appliances at inopportune times, but Anita Gillette was in it so it couldn't have been all bad.

Lancelot Link, Secret Chimp (ABC, 1970–72)

A Saturday morning classic, *Lancelot Link* was a live-action send-up of Maxwell Smart and other superspies, with an all-chimpanzee cast. Lance, agent of APE (Agency to Prevent Evil), battled the bad guys from CHUMP (Criminal Headquarters for Underworld Master Plan). He was assisted by femme fatale Mata Hairi, and reported to Commander Darwin (best line in any episode was Lance to the Commander: "What's your theory, Darwin?"). Fans fondly remember Lance's band the Evolution Revolution, his swank bachelor pad with the secret coffee table entrance, and the rogues gallery, especially Wang Fu and Dr. Strangemind. Voices for the chimps were provided by Dayton Allen, Joan Gerber, and *The Love Boat*'s Bernie Kopell.

The Banana Splits Adventure Hour (NBC, 1968–70)

Bingo the orange gorilla was one of four members of this bizarre animal quartet, that introduced psychedelia to the tots of TV Land, and probably resembled a bad acid trip to their older siblings. Fleegle, Bingo, Drooper, and Snorky performed bubblegum pop songs, introduced cartoons, and ran around bumping into walls. A killer theme song ("One banana two banana three banana four . . .) set the right manic tone for this high-energy romp.

The Monkees (NBC, 1966–68)

People say they monkeyed around, but they also released some of the best pop songs of the 1960s. Micky Dolenz, Davy Jones, Mike Nesmith, and Peter Tork were hired to play a rock and roll band on a TV series inspired by the Beatles's first film, *A Hard Day's Night*. The series blended Marx Brothers-style lunacy with counterculture trappings, and featured some of the first music videos ever broadcast on television. "Last Train to Clarksville," "I'm a Believer," and "Daydream Believer" all went to number one on the Billboard charts, and the show received an Emmy for Best Comedy Series (besting *Bewitched*, *Get Smart*, and *The Andy Griffith Show*).

Magilla Gorilla (ABC, 1964–67)

One of the great baby boomer cartoon themes ("Gorilla for sale . . ."), opened this delightful entry from the Hanna-Barbera stable, which featured the adventures of Magilla, a pet store gorilla, and the store's owner, Mr. Peebles. "Nobody buys gorillas anymore," was the frequent lament of Peebles, but Magilla was purchased almost every week, though he would always be returned by episode's end. *Magilla Gorilla* was one of the first cartoons to be created in conjunction with a toy company, thus paving the way for *Transformers*, *Micronauts*, and other atrocities. Magilla was voiced by Allen Melvin, best known as Sam the Butcher on *The Brady Bunch*.

The Today Show (NBC, 1953–)

In the early days of television, when NBC created *The Today Show*, host Dave Garroway was often visited by a chimpanzee named J. Fred Muggs, which helped boost ratings.

CHAPTER TEN

WHATEVER HAPPENED TO . . .

Mort Abrahams
Writer, *Beneath the Planet of the Apes*
Mort Abrahams switched from writer to producer after *Beneath*. Among his credits: *The Greek Tycoon* (1978), *The House on Garibaldi Street* (1979), and *Seven Hours to Judgment* (1988).

Claude Akins
Aldo, *Battle for the Planet of the Apes*
Claude Akins went from playing a monkey to working with one, in the TV series *BJ and the Bear* (1978–81). His character, the bumbling Sheriff Lobo, proved popular enough to be spun off into his own series, which ran three seasons. He died in 1994.

Lew Ayres
Mandemus, *Battle for the Planet of the Apes*
The extraordinary career of Lew Ayres dates back to the era of silent film. He was nominated for an Academy Award in 1948 for his supporting performance in *Johnny Belinda*, and played Dr. Kildare in a very successful series of MGM medical dramas. After playing Mandemus in *Beneath the Planet of the Apes*, Ayres appeared in *Battlestar: Galactica* (1978), *Damien: Omen II* (1978), and in the *Hart to Hart* reunion movie, *Crimes of the Heart* (1994). He died in 1996.

Richard Blackburn

Dr. Zaius/Bill Hudson, *Return to the Planet of the Apes*
Return to the Planet of the Apes was Richard Blackburn's only foray into animation. He played bit parts and small roles in several films and TV series, such as *Stanley and Iris* (1990), *Murder at 1600* (1997), and the miniseries *Storm of the Century* (1999).

Eric Braeden

Dr. Otto Hasslein, *Escape from the Planet of the Apes*
For three decades, Eric Braeden has played tycoon Victor Newman on the daytime drama *The Young and the Restless*, a role that earned him an Emmy award as Best Actor. Between Newman's many marriages and underhanded business schemes, Braeden has played sinister Germans in such projects as *The New Original Wonder Woman* (1975) and *Herbie Goes to Monte Carlo* (1977). In 1997, he went down with the ship as John Jacob Astor in *Titanic* (1997).

Victor Buono

Fat Man, *Beneath the Planet of the Apes*
The charismatic Victor Buono played the heavy, both literally and figuratively, in dozens of films and television shows, though he's probably still best remembered as the rotund Egyptian supervillain King Tut on the *Batman* series. After *Beneath*, he appeared on the short-lived series *Man from Atlantis* (1977–78), and played President William Taft in the 1979 miniseries *Backstairs at the White House*. Buono died of a heart attack in 1982.

Jeff Burton

Dodge, *Planet of the Apes*
Jeff Burton played small roles in *The Mad Bomber* (1972) and *The President's Plane is Missing* (1973), and appeared opposite Pam Grier in the "blaxploitation" classic *Coffy* (1973). He died in 1988.

John Chambers
Makeup, *Planet of the Apes* film series
John Chambers' makeup wizardry helped create an entire menagerie of odd creatures in such films as *The Island of Dr. Moreau* (1977) and *Halloween II* (1981).

Don Pedro Colley
Negro, *Beneath the Planet of the Apes*
Don Pedro Colley created the role of no-nonsense sheriff "Big Ed" Little from Chickasaw County, on the action series *The Dukes of Hazzard* from 1981 to 1984. He has since appeared in *Cagney and Lacey: The Return* (1994) and Roger Corman's *Piranha* (1995).

Booth Colman
Dr. Zaius, *Planet of the Apes* TV series
Booth Colman played Dr. Watson in Martin Ritt's *Norma Rae* (1979), and appeared in a 1995 episode of *Star Trek: Voyager*. In 2000, he costarred in *Return to the Secret Garden.*

Henry Corden
General Urko, *Return to the Planet of the Apes*
Following his portrayal of General Urko, Henry Corden continued his busy career in voice animation, playing Fred Flintstone in a variety of Hanna-Barbera projects including *Fred Flintstone and Friends* (1977) and *The Jetsons Meet the Flintstones* (1987). His voice can also be heard in *Heathcliff* (1980), *Here Comes Garfield* (1982), and *Challenge of the GoBots* (1984).

Jeff Corey
Caspay, *Beneath the Planet of the Apes*
Jeff Corey played Wild Bill Hickok in the Dustin Hoffman film *Little Big Man* (1970), and appeared opposite Sidney Poitier in *They Call Me Mister Tibbs* (1970). Still one of the busier character actors in movies, Corey's more recent credits include *Bird on a Wire* (1990), *Beethoven's 2nd* (1993), and *Color of Night* (1994).

John William Corrington, Joyce Hooper Corrington
Writers, *Battle For the Planet of the Apes*
After *Battle*, John Corrington collaborated with his wife, Joyce, on *The Arena* (1973) and *The Killer Bees* (1974), and, in 1990, wrote the outstanding television drama *Decoration Day*.

James Daly
Honorius, *Planet of the Apes*
James Daly spent seven years as Dr. Paul Lochner on the series *Medical Center* (1969–76). He died on July 3, 1978. Daly is the father of Tyne Daly (*Cagney and Lacey, Judging Amy*) and Tim Daly (*Wings, The Fugitive*).

Severn Darden
Kolp, *Conquest of the Planet of the Apes*
Severn Darden played Dr. Popesco on *Mary Hartman, Mary Hartman* (1976–78), and its spinoff, *Forever Fernwood* (1977). He played distinguished professors in such films as *Real Genius* (1985) and *Back to School* (1986). He died in 1995.

Paul Dehn
Writer, *Beneath the Planet of the Apes, Escape from the Planet of the Apes, Conquest of the Planet of the Apes*; story, *Battle for the Planet of the Apes*
Paul Dehn's only post-*Apes* credit was his Oscar-nominated screenplay for the film adaptation of Agatha Christie's *Murder on the Orient Express* (1974). He died on September 30, 1976.

Bradford Dillman
Dr. Lewis Dixon, *Escape from the Planet of the Apes*
As Captain Briggs, Bradford Dillman tangled with Dirty Harry (Clint Eastwood) in *The Enforcer* (1976) and *Sudden Impact* (1983), and played Darryl Clayton on the drama series *Falcon Crest* from 1982 to 1983.

Maurice Evans

Dr. Zaius, *Planet of the Apes, Beneath the Planet of the Apes*

Maurice Evans' two signature roles, as Dr Zaius and Samantha's warlock father on *Bewitched* (1964–72), might seem like odd claims to fame for a classically-trained actor who spent years playing Shakespearian roles on the London stage. Evans acted sparingly in the 1970s, in such diverse projects as the horror film *Terror in the Wax Museum* (1973), and Steve Martin's movie debut, *The Jerk* (1979). He died of cancer in East Sussex, England on March 12, 1988.

James Franciscus

Brent, *Beneath the Planet of the Apes*

Though he played other virile leading men like Brent in action movies, James Franciscus found greater success in television. He starred in the series *Longstreet* (1971–72) and *Hunter* (1977). He portrayed President John F. Kennedy in the miniseries *Jacqueline Bouvier Kennedy* (1981), opposite Jaclyn Smith, and played a Kennedy-inspired character in the film *The Greek Tycoon* (1978). Franciscus died of emphysema in 1991.

Jerry Goldsmith

Music composer, *Planet of the Apes, Escape from the Planet of the Apes*

More than 30 years after *Planet of the Apes*, Jerry Goldsmith remains one of Hollywood's busiest film composers. He has scored more than 100 films, including many of the biggest science fiction hits of the past three decades: *Alien* (1979), *Poltergeist* (1982), *Gremlins* (1984), *Supergirl* (1984), *The Mummy* (1999), and *The Hollow Man* (2000). As *Star Trek's* resident composer, Goldsmith wrote the theme to the *Voyager* series, and scored four of the *Trek* films. He has been nominated for the Academy Award 18 times, and won the "Best Score" Oscar for *The Omen* (1976).

Thomas Gomez

Minister, *Beneath the Planet of the Apes*

Beneath the Planet of the Apes was Thomas Gomez's final film appearance in a career that spanned more than 50 films dating back to 1942's *Pittsburgh*. He died in an automobile accident in Santa Monica, California on June 18, 1971.

James Gregory

Ursus, *Beneath the Planet of the Apes*

In 1975, James Gregory began a seven-year stint as the absent-minded Inspector Frank Luger on *Barney Miller* (1975–82). His film work includes performances in *The Main Event* (1979) and *Flight of Dragons* (1982).

Ron Harper

Alan Virdon, *Planet of the Apes* TV series

After *Planet of the Apes* was canceled, Ron Harper braved another hostile wilderness in the excellent Sid and Marty Krofft series *Land of the Lost* (1976–77). He played recurring roles on the series *Capitol* (1982), *Loving* (1983), and *Generations* (1989), and appeared with comedy legends Jack Lemmon and Walter Matthau in *The Odd Couple II* (1998).

(Globe Photos)

Linda Harrison

Nova, *Planet of the Apes*, *Beneath the Planet of the Apes*

Though her name doesn't appear in the credits, Linda Harrison's first film after *Beneath* was *Airport 1975* (1974). Billed as Augusta Summerland, Harrison played Winnie, private secretary to silver screen star Gloria Swanson, who played herself. Charlton Heston, Harrison's former cage-mate on the ape planet, played the pilot who helps save Swanson's airplane. Since then, Harrison's film appearances have been few. She appeared in *Cocoon* (1985) and the sequel *Cocoon: The Return* (1988), and was last seen in *The Runaway Bride* (1999).

Charlton Heston

George Taylor, *Planet of the Apes, Beneath the Planet of the Apes*

Planet of the Apes added another distinguished credit to the prodigious film and stage career of Charlton Heston. His specialty is heroic figures, and after portraying astronaut George Taylor he performed good deeds in *Airport 1975* (1974), *Earthquake* (1974), *Midway* (1976), and *Two-Minute Warning* (1976). Heston played Jason Colby on the *Dynasty* spinoff *The Colbys* (1985–86), and sent up his larger-than-life image in *Wayne's World 2* (1993).

Kim Hunter

Dr. Zira, *Planet of the Apes, Beneath the Planet of the Apes, Escape from the Planet of the Apes*

Television kept Kim Hunter busy after Zira's tragic passing. She was a guest on *Columbo* (1971), *The Magician* (1973), and *Ellery Queen* (1975). Her film credits include *A Price Above Rubies* (1998) with Renee Zellweger, and *Midnight in the Garden of Good and Evil* (1997). More recently, Hunter costarred in *A Smaller Place* (2000) and *Here's to Life!* (2000).

John Huston

Lawgiver, *Battle for the Planet of the Apes*

Though he acted in many films, most notably in Roman Polanski's *Chinatown* (1974), John Huston is best remembered as one of the great directors in the history of motion pictures. His post-*Apes* credits include *The Man Who Would Be King* (1975), *Annie* (1982), and *Prizzi's Honor* (1985). He died in 1987.

Arthur P. Jacobs

Producer, *Planet of the Apes* film series
After the *Apes* series, Arthur Jacobs produced musical adaptations of *Tom Sawyer* (1973) and *Huckleberry Finn* (1974). He died on June 27, 1973.

Gordon Jump

Auctioneer, *Conquest of the Planet of the Apes*
It's hard to find a situation comedy in the 1970s that didn't feature a guest appearance from Gordon Jump. In 1978, he began a five-year run as Arthur "Big Guy" Carlson on WKRP *in Cincinnati* (1978–82). He was also a regular on *Growing Pains* (1985–93) and *Sister Kate* (1989–90), and appeared in commercials as the lonely Maytag repairman.

John Landis

Jake's Friend, *Battle for the Planet of the Apes*
Shortly after his glorified walk-on in *Battle for the Planet of the Apes*, John Landis became one of Hollywood's most successful directors, with credits including *National Lampoon's Animal House* (1978), *The Blues Brothers* (1980), *An American Werewolf in London* (1981), *Trading Places* (1983), and *Coming to America* (1988).

Harry Lauter

General Winthrop, *Escape from the Planet of the Apes*
Bad guys were Harry Lauter's specialty, which he plied mostly in forgettable films such as *The Todd Killings* (1971) and *Superbeast* (1972). He died in 1990.

Mark Lenard

General Urko, *Planet of the Apes* TV series
Mark Lenard reprised his role as Mr. Spock's father, Sarek, in *Star Trek: The Motion Picture* (1979) and three sequels: *The Search for Spock* (1984), *The Voyage Home* (1986), and *The Undiscovered Country* (1991). Lenard died on November 22, 1996.

Cornelius and Zira, together again: Roddy McDowall and Kim Hunter embrace at the 30th anniversary screening of *Planet of the Apes* (Lisa Rose/ Globe Photos).

Roddy McDowall

Cornelius, *Planet of the Apes, Escape from the Planet of the Apes*; Caesar, *Conquest of the Planet of the Apes, Battle for the Planet of the Apes*; Galen, *Planet of the Apes* TV series

As a child star in the Golden Age of Hollywood, Roderick Andrew Anthony Jude McDowall grew up in the movies, and fans grew up watching him. Though he may be best remembered for *Planet of the Apes*, McDowall's credits span every genre of film and television. As horror movie host Peter Vincent in *Fright Night* (1985), McDowall earned critical raves. He lent his distinctive voice to the

Mad Hatter in *Batman: The Animated Series* (1992), and played Mr. Soil in Disney's *A Bug's Life* (1998). On October 3, 1998, in Studio City, California, Roddy McDowall succumbed to cancer.

Edwin Mills
Cornelius, *Return to the Planet of the Apes*
Following his stint as the voice of Cornelius, Edwin Mills completed only one more project, portraying a doctor in the exploitation flick *Mother, Jugs, and Speed* (1976), before his death in 1981.

Sal Mineo
Milo, *Escape from the Planet of the Apes*
A heartthrob in the 1950s after his appearance in *Rebel Without a Cause* (1955) opposite James Dean, Sal Mineo's career was tragically cut short just five years after his appearance in *Escape*, when he was murdered in Los Angeles. His final screen appearance was as himself in the Dean bio *James Dean: The First American Teenager* (1975).

Ricardo Montalban
Armando, *Escape from the Planet of the Apes*, *Conquest of the Planet of the Apes*
Armando was a humble circus owner, quite a departure from the larger than life heroes and villains usually played by Ricardo Montalban. For seven seasons he welcomed actors between jobs to *Fantasy Island* (1978–84), as the mysterious Mr. Roarke. In 1982 he reprised his *Star Trek* role of the malevolent Khan and battled Captain Kirk in *Star Trek II: The Wrath of Khan*. Montalban later starred in the TV series *The Colbys* (1985–86), and bedeviled Leslie Nielsen in the uproarious spoof *The Naked Gun* (1988).

Don Murray
Breck, *Conquest of the Planet of the Apes*
Knots Landing fans may remember Don Murray as Sid Fairgate

(1979–81), but Murray has kept busy in numerous projects since his days as Breck. He appeared in the miniseries *How the West Was Won* (1977), and the films *Endless Love* (1981) and *Peggy Sue Got Married* (1986). More recently, he can be seen in *Elvis Is Alive* (2001).

James Naughton
Pete Burke, *Planet of the Apes* TV series
James Naughton made three more attempts at TV series stardom after *Planet of the Apes* was canceled. He played the Dean of boys in *Making the Grade* (1982), a doctor in 1983's *Trauma Center*, and a struggling single parent in the sitcom *Raising Miranda* (1988). At the movies, Naughton appeared in *The First Wives Club* (1996) and *First Kid* (1996). In the patriotic miniseries *Liberty! The American Revolution* (1997), Naughton played founding father Patrick Henry. Most recently he made a guest appearance on *Ally McBeal* as Ally's father.

Claudette Nevins
Judy Franklin/Nova, *Return to the Planet of the Apes*
Career women are Claudette Nevins's specialty, especially doctors. She wore a white coat in both *Sleeping with the Enemy* (1991), opposite Julia Roberts, and in *Final Vendetta* (1996). She may be best known as Constance Fielding on the popular primetime soap opera *Melrose Place* (1993–98). In 1998, Nevins joined the ranks of *Apes* alumni to join the *Star Trek* universe, when she played a Son'a officer in *Star Trek: Insurrection*.

France Nuyen
Alma, *Battle for the Planet of the Apes*
As Dr. Paulette Kiem, exotic, French-Vietnamese beauty France Nuyen spent three years terrorizing the austere Dr. Craig (William Daniels) on the medical drama *St. Elsewhere* (1986–88). She later appeared in the film adaptation of Amy Tan's *The Joy Luck Club* (1993).

Ted Post

Director, *Beneath the Planet of the Apes*
Among Ted Post's many directorial credits are the Dirty Harry film *Magnum Force* (1973), and the TV series *Ark II* (1976), *B.A.D. Cats* — one of Michelle Pfeiffer's first jobs — (1980), *4 Faces* (1999), and *Old Pals* (2000).

Hari Rhodes

MacDonald, *Conquest of the Planet of the Apes*
Hari Rhodes' post-*Apes* credits include *Roots* (1977), *Coma* (1978), and *Sharky's Machine* (1981). He died in 1992.

Franklin J. Schaffner

Director, *Planet of the Apes*
Planet of the Apes inaugurated an impressive series of directorial assignments for Franklin Schaffner. He won the Academy Award for *Patton* (1970), and directed critical and popular hits *Nicholas and Alexandra* (1971), *Papillon* (1973), and *The Boys from Brazil* (1978). He shepherded Luciano Pavarotti's film debut, *Yes, Giorgio!* in 1982. Schaffner's last credit was the drama *Welcome Home* (1989), starring Kris Kristofferson. He died in 1989.

Rod Serling

Writer, *Planet of the Apes*
Though Rod Serling died in 1975, his brilliant legacy of intelligent, provocative writing for film and television lives on. His "It's a Good Life" screenplay was updated in *Twilight Zone: The Movie* (1983); the 1994 TV movie *The Enemy Within* was based on his 1964 script *Seven Days in May*; the unpublished scripts *In the Presence of Mine Enemies* and *End of the Road* were filmed in 1996 and 1997, respectively, and the 2000 film *A Storm in Summer* was based on a story he wrote in 1970. The original *Twilight Zone* series (1959–64) still airs in syndication, and remains a true television classic.

Planet of the Apes director Franklin Schaffner (CP Picture Archive/ Doug Pizac).

Gregory Sierra

Gorilla Sergeant, *Beneath the Planet of the Apes*

Best known as Detective Chano Amenguale on the television series *Barney Miller* (1975–76), Gregory Sierra was always on TV producers' short lists when they needed a Latino bad guy. Watch for him in reruns of *Columbo*, *Miami Vice*, and *Soap*, among many others. On the big screen, he has appeared in *Honey, I Blew Up the Kid* (1992), *Hot Shots! Part Deux* (1993), and *John Carpenter's Vampires* (1998).

Austin Stoker

MacDonald, *Battle for the Planet of the Apes*; Jeff Carter, *Return to the Planet of the Apes*

Austin Stoker appeared in John Carpenter's cult classic *Assault on Precinct 13* (1976), and in the landmark television miniseries *Roots* (1977). His most recent film appearance was as a security guard in *Two Shades of Blue* (2000).

Don Taylor

Director, *Escape from the Planet of the Apes*

Don Taylor directed *Damien: Omen II* (1978), and several films made for television. For BBC Television Shakespeare, he directed a fine adaptation of *Two Gentlemen of Verona* in 1983. Taylor died in 1998.

J. Lee Thompson

director, *Conquest of the Planet of the Apes*, *Battle For the Planet of the Apes*

After reteaming with *Apes* producer Arthur Jacobs to direct Jacobs' musical adaptation of *Huckleberry Finn* (1974), J. Lee Thompson went on to direct *The Greek Tycoon* (1978), and then began a working partnership with actor Charles Bronson for the films *Caboblanco* (1980), *Ten to Midnight* (1983), *The Evil That Men Do* (1984), *Death Wish 4: The Crackdown* (1987), *Messenger of Death* (1988), and *Kinjite: Forbidden Subjects* (1989).

Natalie Trundy
Albina, *Beneath the Planet of the Apes*; Dr. Stephanie Branton, *Escape from the Planet of the Apes*, Lisa, *Conquest of the Planet of the Apes*, *Battle for the Planet of the Apes*

Natalie Trundy's husband was Arthur Jacobs, which explains why she appeared in four of the *Planet of the Apes* films. After that, she made only one other film appearance, in a 1974 musical adaptation of Mark Twain's *Huckleberry Finn*, which was also produced by Arthur Jacobs.

Lou Wagner
Lucius, *Planet of the Apes*, *Beneath the Planet of the Apes*; busboy in *Conquest of the Planet of the Apes*.

Little Lucius grew up to play police mechanic Harlan on the series *CHiPs* (1978–83). In 1999, he appeared in the film *Starry Night*.

M. Emmet Walsh
Aide, *Escape from the Planet of the Apes*

One of Hollywood's most reliable character actors, the versatile M. Emmet Walsh has appeared in more than 100 films and television shows since 1980. Look for him in *Ordinary People* (1980), *Reds* (1981), *Blade Runner* (1982), *Silkwood* (1983), *Blood Simple* (1984), *Fletch* (1985), *Romeo + Juliet* (1996), *My Best Friend's Wedding* (1997), and *The Wild, Wild West* (1999).

David Watson
Cornelius, *Beneath the Planet of the Apes*

David Watson made guest appearances on *The Bionic Woman* and *Charlie's Angels*, both in 1976. Most of his post-*Apes* work has been on the New York concert stage.

James Whitmore
President of the Assembly, *Planet of the Apes*

Military men are one of James Whitmore's specialty. He was a Captain in *Nobody's Perfect* (1968), an Admiral in *Tora! Tora! Tora!*

James Whitmore went from playing the President of the Assembly in *Planet of the Apes* to President Harry Truman in *Give 'em Hell, Harry!* (1975) (Gale M. Adler/ Globe Photos).

(1970), and a General in *I Will Fight No More Forever* (1975). Whitmore portrayed President Harry S. Truman in *Give 'Em Hell, Harry!* (1975), and author Mark Twain in *The Adventures of Mark Twain* (1985). In 2000, he had a reunion of sorts with Kim Hunter in *Here's to Life!*

Paul Williams
Virgil, *Battle for the Planet of the Apes*
Diminutive, Oscar-winning composer Paul Williams was also a busy actor in the 1970s and 1980s. He appeared in *Smokey and the Bandit* (1977) and its two sequels, and *The Muppet Movie* (no, not as a muppet) in 1979. Williams has been a guest star on *Star Trek: Voyager* (1995), and has provided the voice of the Penguin in *Batman: The Animated Series* (1992).

Michael Wilson
Writer, *Planet of the Apes*
Blacklisted in the 1950s during the Communist witchhunts spearheaded in congress by Senator Joseph McCarthy, writer Michael Wilson did not receive credit for his most famous work until decades after his retirement. Wilson wrote *It's a Wonderful Life* (1946), *A Place in the Sun* (1951), *Friendly Persuasion* (1956), *Bridge on the River Kwai* (1957), and *Lawrence of Arabia* (1962), classics all. His final script was for 1969's *Che!*, starring Jack Palance. He died in 1978.

William Windom
The President, *Escape from the Planet of the Apes*
William Windom has made guest appearances on dozens of television series, such as *Knight Rider* (1982), *Murder She Wrote* (1984), *L.A. Law* (1986), *Murphy Brown* (1988), and *Judging Amy* (1999). His film credits include *Planes, Trains & Automobiles* (1987), *Sommersby* (1993), and *True Crime* (1999).

CHAPTER ELEVEN

2001:
An Apes Odyssey

You think Taylor's spacecraft took a few wrong turns before landing in our ape-dominated future? That's nothing compared to the road traveled by the remake of *Planet of the Apes*. But after ten years, four directors, and too many writers to count (and let's face it, you don't count writers in Hollywood anyway), the apes are finally back in the nation's theaters, in what has become *the* big summer movie of 2001. As with any remake of a classic, expectations are high, and there is much trepidation among some fans that perhaps we should have just left well enough alone. But, as Cornelius said to Zira in *Escape from the Planet of the Apes*, there's no going back now. (Well, he *probably* said it in the rocket, we just didn't see it).

The journey began back in 1992, when New Zealand director Peter Jackson (*Heavenly Creatures*) pitched the idea for a new *Apes* film to Twentieth Century Fox. Similar pitches from uncredited writers and fans had arrived at a steady trickle almost since the cancellation of the *Apes* television series in 1974. All of them were deposited directly in the round metal file under the desk of studio chief Joe Roth, who had no interest in reviving the franchise.

But by 1992 Roth had departed to Disney, and the studio was now controlled by executives who had grown up watching the original, and were also excited by the idea of a remake. They

Director Tim Burton poses with Linda Harrison and her family on the set of *Planet of the Apes* (2001). From left: Burton, Patricia Zanuck, Harrison Zanuck, Linda Harrison, Dean Francis Zanuck (Courtesy Linda Harrison).

passed on Jackson's idea, but in December of 1993 they gave the green light to producers Don Murphy and Jane Hamsher, albeit with two non-negotiable conditions: first, that director Oliver Stone be attached as executive producer; second, that the new movie would have nothing to do with the previous series of films, but instead take as its source Pierre Boulle's *Monkey Planet*. Writer Terry Hayes (*The Road Warrior*, *Dead Calm*) was hired to pen the script.

The result was a radical revamping of both Boulle's novel and the entire concept of a futuristic parable. Co-producer Don Murphy described it as "*Gorillas in the Mist* meets *The Terminator*." "I know there are a lot of fans of the original film series out there, and that they will be offended — but if you watch those films, they're dated."

Hayes chose to set his *Planet of the Apes* in the distant past, where a scientist travels back to a primitive era in man's evolution when the earth was ruled by an ancient ape culture. "Our (version) is set in *Quest for Fire* times, the dawn of man," said producer Jane Hamsher in 1994. "It has very biblical, mythic overtones." The scientist's journey is prompted by an epidemic of stillborn human babies, which are the result of a DNA defect spawned from our ape ancestors.

Before a first draft was completed, Kenner Toys had already signed on to create the merchandise tie-ins, and Rick Baker was hired to create the apes. Baker revealed his intent to model the simians in the new film after the apes he created for *Greystoke: The Legend of Tarzan* (1984). These would be full gorilla, chimpanzee, and orangutan costumes, without the integration of human features.

Stone convinced Arnold Schwarzenegger to play the scientist, pending the choice of director. But Fox wasn't happy with the script, or with Stone's projected budget of $100 million. Rewrites were requested, to remove some of the techno-babble and make the story more family-friendly. Philip Noyce (*Patriot Games*) was approved by Stone and Schwarzenegger as director, but after the first script was tossed Noyce skipped to do *The Saint* (1998), and Ah-nuld left to shoot *Eraser* (1998).

In 1995, Stone, Murphy, and Hamsher's "dawn of man" concept was abandoned, following their departure from the project. Fox asked director Chris Columbus (*Gremlins, Home Alone*) to rewrite the script with Sam Hamm (*Batman*), and tried to interest James Cameron (*True Lies, Titanic*) in producing. Columbus collaborated with makeup man Stan Winston to create some incredible ape facial mechanicals that the studio eagerly approved. But before the year was out, Cameron passed, and Columbus and Schwarzenegger teamed up to make *Jingle All the Way* (1996). Winston's special effects creations were later adapted by director Ron Howard for use by Jim Carrey in *Dr. Seuss's How the Grinch Stole Christmas* (2000).

Mark Wahlberg plays the astronaut on a strange new world in the 2001 remake of *Planet of the Apes* (CP Picture Archive/ Rick Maiman).

After *Independence Day* became *the* event movie of 1996, Fox offered its *Apes* remake to *ID:4* director Roland Emmerich, who expressed his preference for reptiles by making *Godzilla* (1997) instead. The studio then approached Peter Jackson again, but he accepted a better offer from Universal to satisfy his simian cravings with a remake of *King Kong*. Meanwhile, the script passed through another draft by Andrew Kevin Walker in 1999, and Michael Bay (*Armageddon*) also turned down the director's chair.

It was beginning to look like *Planet of the Apes* was a can't-miss movie that nobody wanted to make. Finally, the first piece fell into place in 1998, when writer William Broyles (*Apollo 13, Cast Away*) delivered a workable script, that returned the concept to more familiar terrain — lost astronauts, time travel, social commentary, and damn dirty apes. The script found its way to director Tim Burton, already a master at putting a kinky spin on familiar stories (*Batman, Sleepy Hollow*). Fans couldn't ask for a better man at the helm, and sounded the ram's horn from coast to coast when Burton agreed to direct.

The rumor mill began churning in early 2000, but the first accurate leaks didn't trickle out until late summer: Mark Wahlberg (*Boogie Nights, The Perfect Storm*) would play the lead human character (a role originally offered to Matt Damon), an astronaut who travels 2000 years into earth's past, on the trail of a previously-launched spacecraft carrying a genetically-altered gorilla. He lands on a familiar-looking planet, in an area dubbed the Forbidden Zone, and finds the gorilla being worshipped as a deity. As the astronaut struggles with questions of which species evolved from which, his quest for answers leads to a stunning finale — one that Burton promised would carry the same dramatic impact as the Statue of Liberty's appearance in the 1968 film. However, Wahlberg's contract contained a sequel clause, so whatever else happens, he can be expected to survive the shock ending.

Other human characters would be played by Kris Kristofferson and Estella Warren. Cast as ape leads were Michael Clarke Duncan, Tim Roth, Helena Bonham-Carter, Paul Giamatti, Glenn Shadix, and Burton's main squeeze Lisa Marie, who has appeared in every Burton film since the couple hooked up during *Ed Wood* (1994). Gary Oldman was originally signed to play the top Gorilla baddie, but later departed in a huff, calling the producers "cheap." Charlton Heston and Linda Harrison would make cameos, as would George Clooney, who costarred with Wahlberg in *Three Kings* (1999) and *The Perfect Storm* (2000).

Rick Baker, who was first contacted about an *Apes* remake in 1994, assembled a team of 75 makeup artists to turn 500 actors

The lovely face of Helena Bonham-Carter will be hidden
beneath layers of latex, for her role as ape princess Ari
(CP Picture Archive/ Kevork Djansezian).

and extras into chimpanzees, gorillas, and orangutans. Other
simian species will also be featured, such as baboons, mandrills,
and spider monkeys. A specialized latex, foam rubber compound
was used for the ape masks. Known as McLaughlin Foam in the
film industry, it had previously been used in the original *Star
Wars* trilogy.

Filming began November 6, 2000, near Lake Powell, (which is
180 miles from the Utah/Arizona border, where the opening
scenes of the 1967 film were shot), and continued in Sun Valley,
California and Hawaii. Spies reported seeing Asiatic, Genghis

**Michael Clarke Duncan plays Attar the ape
warrior in *Planet of the Apes* (2001)
(Gary Marshall/ Shooting Star).**

Khan-style armor on the ape warriors, and walking, talking apes
that looked frighteningly authentic.

The first really juicy gossip to emerge from the production
was of a relationship between astronaut Wahlberg and the ape
played by Helena Bonham-Carter. Nervous Fox executives nixed
the romance, citing the obvious icky overtones of inter species

dating. This and other controversial story elements prompted yet another script rewrite. The job went to Lawrence Konner and Mark Rosenthal, the keyboard peckers behind such bombs as *Superman IV* (1987) and *Mercury Rising* (1999). Fans trying to trust Tim Burton's judgment are having their loyalty tested by a decision that is the cinematic equivalent of having Jackie Collins punch up Tom Wolfe.

A title change to *The Visitor* was considered, and then abandoned for the more recognizable *Planet of the Apes*. Fox hoped to have the film ready for July 4 (traditionally the most prestigious opening weekend of the summer), but the U.S. release date was moved to July 27, 2001.

How will the new *Planet of the Apes* fare? Fans are cautiously optimistic. "It's fun just to see *Apes* in the spotlight again," says Jeff Krueger. "The new 'apeteur,' Tim Burton, is no dummy and he's very pop culture savvy. He's expressed his admiration for *Apes* and probably knows better than most top directors what makes it tick."

"I'm looking forward to the movie, and as a fan of Tim Burton, I'm glad he got the gig," said collector Ken Taylor. "What I do not expect, is whatever twigged in my 12-year-old mind when I first experienced *Planet of the Apes*. If my expectations are too high, I can only be disappointed. I do hope to be pleasantly surprised." Adds "Apeman" Anthony James, "I will love the movie no matter what. It will be a *Planet of the Apes* film, how could you not?"

CHAPTER TWELVE

FOR MORE INFORMATION . . .

Founded by Terry Hoknes in 1991, the International *Planet of the Apes* Fan Club has members in ten different countries. The club publishes *Ape Chronicles*, a fanzine featuring information about every aspect of the *Planet of the Apes* phenomenon. Regular features include Ape Encyclopedia (an A–Z listing of every character in the mythos), Theories on Time (fans' opinions on the time structure of the *Apes* chronology), and Classifieds.

For information on membership rates, contact:

Terry Hoknes
739 Taylor Street East
Saskatoon, Saskatchewan
Canada, S7H 1W1
www.dlcwest.com

Planet of the Apes Web sites:
Ape Fest: The Ultimate in *Planet of the Apes*
www.geocities.com/Hollywood/1170/

Apes Rule Again!
www.foxhome.com/planetoftheapes/frameset.html

Planet of the Apes
http://www.spleenworld.com/apes/

Planet of the Apes Fansite
www.prophecysite.com/

Planet of the Apes International Fan Club
www.dlcwest.com/~comicsape/apes.htm

Planet of the Apes Movie Pages
www.movieprop.com/tvandmovie/PlanetoftheApes/

Planet of the Apes Photo Gallery
www.well-rounded.com/games/reviews/apes_pre.html

Planet of the Apes: The Forbidden Zone
members.xoom.com/planetofapes/index.html

The *Planet of the Apes* Webring Homepage
come.to/ape/

Those Damned Dirty Apes! A *Planet of the Apes* Retrospective
www.geocities.com/aleong1631/pota.html

BIBLIOGRAPHY

BOOKS

Heston, Charlton. *The Actor's Life: Journals 1956–76*. New York: E.P. Dutton, 1976.

Heston, Charlton. *In the Arena*. New York: Simon & Schuster, 1995.

Madsen, Axel. *John Huston*. New York: Doubleday, 1978.

Pratley, Gerald. *The Cinema of John Huston*. New York: A.S. Barnes & Co., 1977.

Zinman, David. *Fifty Grand Movies of the 1960s and 1970s*. New York: Crown, 1986.

MAGAZINES

Clark, Champ, ". . . talking with Charlton Heston." *People*, Sept. 7, 1998.

Gross, Edward. "Welcome Back to the *Planet of the Apes*." *Comics Scene*, June, 1990.

Rieff, David. "What Planet Are We On?" *American Movie Classics*, Sept., 1998.

Russo, Joe, with Larry Landsman and Edward Gross. "*Planet of the Apes Revisited*." *Starlog #105*, Apr., 1986.

Thompson, Anne. "The Apes of Wrath: Anatomy of a Remake." *Entertainment Weekly*, May 10, 1996.

Vaughn, J.C. "A Writer on the *Planet of the Apes*." *Comic Book Marketplace*, May, 1999.

Webb, Gordon C. "30 Years Later: Rod Serling's *Planet of the Apes*." *Creative Screenwriting*, July–Aug., 1998.

Williams, David E. "Oliver's *Apes*." *Sci-Fi Universe*, July, 1994.